"DO YOU WANT TO DO SOMETHING SOMETIME? Like maybe one night this weekend?"

I nodded. "Um, maybe." I probably should have just said no, straight off the bat, but I didn't have a reason to give if he asked. "Why not?" Not a reason I felt comfortable telling him, anyway.

Except for this flock of nervous butterflies in my tummy, it sounded really good. But I couldn't get together with Jackson until I talked it over with Lucy—and if I told Lucy I was interested in him, she'd tell me to stay away from him.

I didn't even know if I *could* walk away.

Also by Catherine Clark

Picture Perfect

Banana Splitsville

Rocky Road Trip

Wish You Were Here

Icing on the Lake

The Alison Rules

Maine Squeeze

Love and Other Things I'm Bad At

Unforgettable Summer

How to Meet Boys

CATHERINE CLARK

HARPER TEEN

An Imprint of HarperCollinsPublishers

HarperTeen is an imprint of HarperCollins Publishers.

How to Meet Boys
Copyright © 2014 by Catherine Clark

Library of Congress Cataloging-in-Publication Data
Clark, Catherine, 1962-
  How to meet boys / Catherine Clark. — First edition.
    pages cm
  Summary: "Best friends Lucy and Mikayla are ready for the best summer of
their lives, but when Mikayla falls for a boy from Lucy's past they realize their
perfect summer might be over before it starts"— Provided by publisher.
  ISBN 978-0-06-226451-0 (pbk.)
  [1. Best friends—Fiction. 2. Friendship—Fiction. 3. Dating (Social customs)—
Fiction. 4. Resorts—Fiction. 5. Family life—Minnesota—Fiction. 6. Minnesota—
Fiction.] I. Title.
PZ7.C5412Hr 2014   2013038561
[Fic]—dc23   CIP
                                                                     AC

Typography by Lissi Erwin
14 15 16 17 18 LP/RRDH 10 9 8 7 6 5 4 3 2 1

First Edition

CHAPTER 1

Lucy

"Is this it?"

"This can't be it."

Mikayla and I climbed out of my car and stood in the gravel driveway.

It was June 10, our summer vacation had started two and a half days ago, and we'd just driven three hours from Minneapolis to stand outside what was supposed to be our dream house for the summer.

"The pictures your grandmother sent made it look a lot better," Mikayla commented.

I had to agree. The small cabin was painted dark red and had white shutters on a few of the windows—while a few other shutters were hanging off, and one had already fallen to the ground. Pine trees surrounded the house, not letting much sunlight through, and I noticed as I got closer that the paint was peeling in a few places.

The screen door practically came off its hinges when I opened it. I removed the envelope taped to the door, and inside was a short note from my grandparents, along with the house key.

WELCOME TO BRIDGEPORT! my grandmother had written in all caps.

We don't have a name for this place yet—hoping you girls will think of one as the summer goes on. We know the place needs a little work—we've given it a fresh paint job inside, and we'll help you find more furniture. We're excited to have you here!

XXOO Nana & G

"Should we go in?" asked Mikayla.

"I guess so. Here goes nothing," I said as I slid the key into the lock. It didn't work at first, so I rattled the doorknob a few times until the door swung open—*fell* open is more like it.

We walked into a narrow entryway beside a tiny coat closet. I flipped on the lights and saw the living room, dining room, and kitchen all in one glance. We wandered down a hallway that led to the bathroom and two bedrooms, one with two single beds and one with a double bed.

"Well, it's small," said Mikayla as we walked back out to the kitchen, "but it's cute small."

"My mother would call it 'cozy charm,'" I said, making air quotes. "Rustic cabin with authentic fireplace and huge heart. Massive potential!" I laughed, half at the house and half at the fact I was quoting my mother's real estate language.

Mikayla ran her fingers along the kitchen counter, which was made of some prehistoric tile material—in brown. "We can make it look better," she said. "We just need to invest in some cute accessories."

The small town where my grandparents live and have an apple orchard is in northern Minnesota. I love everything about Bridgeport, from its old-fashioned street signs to the lakeside cafés. I even love the slow-moving traffic, as long as I'm not the one driving in it.

But this house? I wasn't so sure.

I poked around the kitchen. My grandparents had furnished the place sparingly, with some dishes, a coffeemaker, a well-used toaster oven, and dish towels. In the living room there was a flowered upholstered chair that I remembered from my grandparents' porch—the faded material was a give-away—and two folding beach chairs, with an upside-down cardboard box for a coffee table and a couple of floor lamps that also looked like castoffs.

The rest was going to be up to us, or we could spend the summer living in what looked like the set from a depressing one-act play. That no one would ever go see.

There was no TV, but Mikayla and I both had our computers, so if we could ever get Wi-Fi here, we'd be set . . . but right now I wasn't counting on that. Instead, I figured I'd be doing a lot of reading over the summer, which was fine with me. I wanted to get ahead in a couple of my fall AP classes and be ready for the college-level courses I'd take in the winter and spring. Plus, there were college applications to think about, essays to write . . . Why did I suddenly get the feeling this was going to be an Abraham Lincoln summer? Me, a candle, a pen, some paper . . . and a brilliant speech that I could trot out when I became valedictorian.

Ha ha ha ha ha ha.

I usually visited every summer for a week or two, came on long weekends occasionally, and spent a few Christmas vacations here, when the bay would freeze and you could actually drive on it. But this summer, for the first time ever, I was moving here for two and a half months.

Mikayla and I were living completely on our own, but of course we'd had to swear on our lives to be responsible in every way, as if we weren't all the time anyway. We were practically saints, if you want to know the truth.

Of course, there was no rule that we had to behave exactly the same here as we did at home.

"Which is going to be my room?" asked Mikayla.

"I don't know." We stood in the doorways of each bedroom, surveying the spaces. "Do you want the bigger bed?" I asked.

"No, you take it," Mikayla said. She flopped onto one of the single beds. "Hey, this is pretty comfy."

I walked through the living room and onto the small deck off the back of the house. The view from there was incredible and explained why my grandparents had bought this place. You could see down to the harbor below. "Mikayla, come out here!" I called.

She hurried out the sliding door from the living room. "Now this is what I'm talking about."

"No, it's what *I* was talking about on the way up." I laughed. "My nana said, 'It's not much, but there's a view.' She was right on both counts."

We went back outside to start unpacking the car. The first thing we had to do was remove our bicycles from the car rack, and then take off the rack so we could open the back of my small SUV. Once we got that done, we hauled the boxes out of the back, along with a couple of suitcases of clothes and a few duffel bags.

"You want a ride to the beach club in a while?" I asked, as I carried a desk lamp in one hand and a blow-dryer in the other. "I want to go see my grandparents." Neither of us would start work for a few days—we'd wanted to get to town early and spend a few days settling into the place.

Mikayla set down a bag of oranges on the kitchen counter. "I think I'm going to go for a bike ride, visit the Club, and meet Sarah. I told her we were getting to town today and she said I could drop by for a tour. I could use the exercise after being in the car for so long. Plus, I need to make sure I can find the place, right?"

"You remember where it is, though," I said.

"Pretty much," she said. "It's the getting back *here* part I'm not sure about. Is this technically the woods, or the forest?"

I laughed. "You're such a city kid. It's Hemlock Hill Road. If you remember that, you can find your way back here. Look at the lake, and then head, you know, up the hill."

She squinted at me. "Are you making fun of me?"

"Maybe," I said.

"You're the one who almost got back on the highway heading the wrong direction," Mikayla said as she sorted things in the kitchen, putting away the small sets of plates and glasses she'd picked up at a Goodwill: some matched and some didn't, but they all looked really cool together. "Not me."

We both started laughing and she handed me a filtered pitcher to fill with water. "Can I help it if I get confused by lunch?" I said, running the cold water a bit. Suddenly the faucet made a loud clanking noise and went from running, to spraying randomly, and back to running smoothly again.

"This place is going to be interesting, isn't it?" Mikayla asked, eyeing the sink.

"Let's hope so," I said, wiping water off my forehead with my sleeve. "We didn't drive two hundred miles to be bored."

I was heading to the Apple Store later that afternoon when it happened.

Not *that* Apple Store, where customers line up outside whenever a new iPhone, iPad, or other cool iProduct is released. No, this was The Original Apple Store, which was owned by my grandparents and sold real apples. Crunchy ones. Tart ones. Sweet ones. McIntosh, Cortland, Haralson, Honeycrisp, Northern Spy, Prairie Spy, Rome, and so on.

My job wasn't to know the apples in stock. That was for whoever worked at the Apple Genius Bar. (My grandparents were hoping to get sued by Apple, for the free publicity. They even had a bumper sticker that said *iApple—Do You?* with their store logo on it. They're begging to be caught, and when they go to jail, I'll visit them. Hopefully the trial will be in California, where Apple is based, because I've always wanted to go there.)

Anyway, it's apples versus oranges.

Literally.

My grandparents go a little crazy with the decorations. One is an apple and an orange on different sides of a scale and the headline *You can't compare them—don't even try!*

My grandparents had hired me because they said they needed "reliable" help. Last summer's teen hires had been a disaster, so they'd started begging me as far back as last Christmas. When I resisted, they'd thrown in a house. (And by *house*, I mean that rundown cabin we'd just seen for the first time.)

My parents wouldn't let me live up here on my own, so I'd invited my friends Mikayla and Ava to come with me. Unfortunately, Ava's mother thought it was time for her to have a "serious" job that might help her get into college, so Ava had pursued a few internships and ended up with one at a fashion and arts magazine based in Chicago. I was happy for her, because she really wanted to be in a city—but I was disappointed she couldn't come up here to stay with me and Mikayla.

My grandmother had helped Mikayla find a job at the Bridgeport Beach Club. (When I asked why we couldn't work together at the Apple Store, Nana had said, "The two of you would have too much fun—you wouldn't get anything done.")

Mikayla definitely got the better deal. Not only did the Bridgeport Beach Club pay more, but it was also a very cool place to work because of the big group of people our age working at the Club. I was probably crazy for *not* trying to get a job there. When I started smelling like apples, no doubt I'd regret the decision.

Still, the Apple Store was a lot better than what I did the summer before. I worked at the Mall of America in a coffee chain that had four locations inside the mall. The managers rotated us from store to store, like we were car tires that needed to be switched every ten thousand coffees.

You couldn't have a sharper contrast. I was going from listening to shrieking people on roller coasters and other neon-colored rides twisting upside down above my head—and I can't stand rides—and parking ramps as big as an entire city and endless levels of food courts . . . to this peaceful summer resort town perched on a bay beside one of the Great

Lakes. I took a deep breath of the fresh northern air.

Yes, I was going to enjoy this, I thought as I turned to enter the store.

As my foot hit the first step, someone walked out.

I looked up—and up and up, he was tall—and nearly tripped on the second step. It wasn't just any guy. It was Jackson Rolfsmeier. Sure, his hair was a little longer than the last time I'd seen him, and he was about six inches taller, but he was still the same boy I'd kissed, or tried to kiss, back in eighth grade, only to have him say, "Um, no," and run away. It felt like a century ago, but at the same time it could have been a couple of weeks, considering how nervous and embarrassed I felt even now, three years later.

Jackson was holding the door open for me, waiting for me to come in.

My pulse immediately doubled. Then tripled.

I hadn't seen Jackson up close in about three years, since the kiss incident and the rumors that floated around after it. Once or twice the summer before this one, I'd seen him in town, but I crossed to the other side of the street to avoid him. I was mature like that. But it just didn't make sense to make small talk.

We didn't hate each other. We just . . . well, it was awkward. The way it can be when you go through something really, really embarrassing with a person.

"Hi," he sort of grunted out of the side of his mouth. "Lucy."

It came out as two different thoughts, like he couldn't combine the two. He could say "Hi" and he could say "Lucy," but not together. That might break some unwritten law boys had about acknowledging girls.

I looked up at him. Since when did he have a low voice like that? He sounded like he could do voiceovers for a movie trailer.

He had the same brown hair but it was longer, reminding me of a scruffy Liam Hemsworth. As I stepped up, I realized he had a good half foot on me, height-wise. When did he get so tall? I wished I weren't at such a height disadvantage for such an awkward conversation.

"Oh, hey," I said, pushing my hair back with my hand, the way my mom is always saying I shouldn't do because it's "a tic." Tic, schmick. My hair gets in my eyes sometimes. I didn't have anything else to say, really. My brain was too busy trying to figure out why this had to be the first thing that happened this summer. It felt like a bad omen. *Um, you haven't talked to me in three years. And I haven't talked to you, either. Why are you even saying hi? Did something fall on your head?*

So I just walked into the store and Jackson let the door close behind me, and he went on his way, and I was in the store and that was that.

Except . . . there was something I realized as the door closed.

Jackson was wearing an Original Apple Store staff T-shirt, which could mean only one thing. We were going to be working together.

We're going to be working together. This was the other so-called responsible teen my grandmother had found? *Him?*

CHAPTER 2

Mikayla

One of my favorite things about being in Bridgeport was the fresh air. It smelled like pine trees combined with—nothing at all. A candle could only dream of being that cleanly fragrant. This wasn't something you could re-create with wax and perfume. I'd been in town only a few hours but already I felt like I was healthier—probably because I was riding my bike instead of sitting in traffic on a city bus, or jammed into our minivan with siblings fighting all around me.

I'd been here only a few times before: once on a camping trip in fifth grade, and once last summer when Lucy invited me and Ava up for a few days at her grandparents' place. We'd had such a good time, cruising around town on bikes, kayaking, swimming, making s'mores, and doing all that outdoorsy stuff you do in a northern, remote place like Bridgeport.

I rode my mountain bike down the original historic cobblestone street through the middle of town, the bike tires bouncing on every square, it seemed. I passed a couple of coffee shops, art studios, restaurants, and gift shops that lined the street beside the lake. People were wandering on sidewalks, shopping, while workers placed chalkboard signs listing daily specials outside their cafés. I smelled something delicious baking at the small Swedish bakery as I rode past it. A girl outside the kite store was holding up a bright orange and green kite, and I glanced up to watch the breeze catch it and pull it up high over the water.

I completely missed the stop sign in front of me.

However, I did not miss seeing a small silver car headed across the intersection right at me! Just in time, I managed to swerve off toward the lake side of the road—while the car swerved in the other direction.

I couldn't stop and plowed right into a primrose bush. At least I think that's what it's called. Whatever it was grows near the water and has thorns—many, many thorns. I tumbled to the ground, feeling scratches on my legs, my arms, everywhere.

"Ow. *Ow!*" I gasped.

"I'm so sorry. Are you okay?" a voice called to me.

I pulled myself off my bike and untangled myself from the bush branches. When I came out of the scratchy mess, I saw a boy waiting for me. He looked like he was about my age, or maybe a little older. He had dark brown hair with strong dark eyebrows, and he was wearing a faded orange retro T-shirt and khaki shorts. He looked sort of preppy.

"That was horrible of me," he said. "I'm—I can't believe I almost hit you."

"No, my fault—it was," I said. "The stop sign . . . I didn't see." Why was I talking like Yoda from *Star Wars*? I cannot talk to boys at all. It's just a fact. I could take all the energy and talent I have when I'm giving pep talks to my teammates and all the skill I have when it comes to taking chemistry exams or speaking Spanish and just crumple it up into a ball when a boy who's even slightly cute in any way at all is around.

"Wow. I'm lucky no one else was around. I mean, if any other cars were coming—or people—are you okay? Really?" He stepped closer to me again, and I couldn't help noticing that compared to the boys I usually attempted talking to, he was a lot nicer, especially the way he kept worrying about me.

I nodded and gave what I hoped was a charming smile.

"You—you don't look okay," he said.

"Thanks," I muttered under my breath. My forehead was stinging, so I reached up to touch it. My hand came away with blood on it. My arm was scratched in several places and bleeding, too. Well, at least I'd been wearing a helmet. *Look on the bright side, Mikayla*, I thought to myself. *You didn't break anything, like your head. Just your ego.*

"Need some help?" he asked. "I'm like—I don't have any tissues but I might have a towel in the car—"

"Oh, uh, no," I said, thinking of what kind of icky towel he'd pull out from under the seat. "I'm fine."

"Are you sure?" he asked.

"Yeah—I'm sure." I'd been in bike crashes before. I'd competed in mini triathlons. I knew how to get up. I wished I could just say that more nicely, instead of barking at him.

He looked sort of stunned. Hey, it's a reaction I get from boys sometimes. I can't help it. "Fine. If you say so. You look pretty bad."

"Thanks, really." As I untangled my bike from the shrubbery, I saw another big scratch on my leg and a smear of bike grease on my ankle. So complementary.

"I feel terrible, though. You could have been really hurt." He tried to give me a piece of paper, and I noticed his hand was shaking. "Here," he said. "You want my number? In case you have to go to the doctor or—"

"I won't need to go to the doctor." Did he think I was made out of china or porcelain or something fragile like that?

"You never know. I'm just saying . . . maybe you should get checked out?"

"Maybe," I said, just to make him feel better. "But I don't even have a doctor here. I don't even, like, live here, so I wouldn't even know where to go," I babbled. Gah! Too much information. "I promise you, I'm fine. And you know what? I'm late."

I adjusted my helmet, climbed onto my bike, and rode off toward the Bridgeport Beach Club. Why did I have to get into an accident on my first day in town? And why did it have to be with Mr. Cute Car Driver?

I glanced over my shoulder for a second and saw him pulling away in his silver VW Jetta.

He'd tried to give me his number, and I'd refused. Despite the fact that I found him completely cute and that he was quite possibly the nicest guy who had ever talked to me, if you didn't count people who were saying things like "Nice game" and "Spike it, Mikayla!" Guys cheered for me at volleyball matches and in track. That was different.

What was wrong with me? No guy had ever offered me his number before. Unless you count the coach for St. Augustine Academy, our biggest rival, and I definitely do not. He was only trying to recruit me. That does *not* count.

I quickly rode the last few miles out to the Club, but was stopped at the entrance gate by a security guard.

"Hudson, Hudson . . . let's see. You're here to check in? I don't have a special note about it and your name is not on this list."

I sighed. What kind of place was this? I needed a special note just to get in? Of course, I kind of knew that about the Club. It was exclusive. Right now I was on the outside, the "ex" side of things.

"I'm a summer employee. I don't officially start until Thursday, so I don't have a keycard yet," I explained. "That's the problem."

"But you're not on my list," he said.

"Well, then it's a mistake," I argued. "How about if you call my supervisor, Sarah?"

The boy working the security gate shook his head. He had blond hair that was so short he could have been in the military. He was wearing a blue BBC polo shirt—the kind I'd have to wear—and leaning his elbows on the window of the little booth.

The collar of his shirt was folded up in that preppy way and the shirt color matched his eyes perfectly. He was too neat. That made me not trust him. You could tell that he really liked being the one who got to turn people away. He was a born hall monitor.

"I'll call her, but do you have an ID on you?" he asked. "Because I can't let you in without verifying who you are first."

I dug in my back pocket for my wallet. This was ridiculous. We were talking about a beach club, not an international flight. What did he think I was, a terrorist?

Still, I thought, handing him my driver's license, I guess that was part of the appeal of the Club. You didn't show up at a place called Bridgeport Beach Club and expect it *not* to be that way. Everyone who came through the gate needed a special ID pass, and there was no talking your way around it.

I would know. I had tried it the summer before when I was visiting Lucy at her grandparents'. All I wanted was a place to go to the bathroom. I was out on a long training run and sometimes a person just needs to make a pit stop. But no, not at "the Club," as everyone called it. You'd be turned away, probably even in a thunderstorm with deadly lightning.

It wasn't a country club, exactly. But it was darned close.

You had to live within certain town boundaries to have access to the beach, buildings, tennis courts, shuffleboard courts, nine-hole golf course, wine bar, swimming pool— and you had to pay monthly dues, too.

"I can't reach her." He handed me back my license. "But I wrote down your info, so if you try to make off with any of the silverware or statues or anything, they'll be able to find you."

"I wouldn't—take—" I stammered.

"I'm kidding. I'm Liam, by the way. And do you have a number or a local address I can write down here? 'Cause I assume you're not planning to ride up from Minneapolis every morning," he said.

I laughed and gave him my cell number. I heard a car honk and glanced behind me. There was a short line of cars waiting to go through the security gate. "I should go," I said. "See you later." I started walking my bike toward the main building.

"Hold on, hold on. Mikayla!" Liam called after me.

I stopped and looked over my shoulder.

"What happened to your leg?" he asked, leaning way out of the booth.

"Oh—it's nothing," I said, glancing down.

"Nothing?" He pointed at my shin. "You're bleeding and you have chain marks."

"I—a bike accident," I said.

"You should go to the nurse's station. It's just past the spa," he called after me.

"Thanks!" I yelled over my shoulder. He was so nice—not at all like my first impression.

"Yeah. Get some Band-Aids. That looks disgusting!" he shouted after me.

I don't meet boys well. At all. It's just a fact.

CHAPTER 3

Lucy

I found my grandmother in her little office behind the sales counter.

"Lucy! You finally made it!" she cried. "What did you do, drive here by way of Canada?"

Get lost once, and your family will never forget it. Was it my fault the signs made it seem like Bridgeport was north of the Canadian border? I'd only gotten my license about a month earlier, and I didn't want to check my phone while I was driving; I'd been drilled about not doing that for two years straight, even before they'd let me get my learner's permit.

Some people would say I'm directionally challenged. *Some* people.

"It's so good to see you, Nana!" I gave her a warm hug.

"You too," she replied. "Claire dropped by about an hour ago, looking for you. I told her to stop back a little bit later."

I smiled. I couldn't wait to catch up in person with Claire Bannon. I'd known her for years, because she lived in the house down the road from my grandparents' farm. She lived year-round in Bridgeport, which had a much smaller winter population, and we usually hung out whenever I was visiting.

I'd been in touch with her *and* my grandparents a lot lately, getting the details for the summer nailed down—or trying to. My grandmother wasn't big on details. You had to pull things out of her, like what the cabin was like, and when your first day at work would be, and—

Speaking of which, I had a question for her. "Nana. Is Jackson Rolfsmeier working here this summer?"

"Yes, he is." She tapped a few numbers into the adding machine on her wooden desk and smiled at me. "He started today, just for a couple of hours. Breaking him in gently."

What was he, a horse? "Today? Really?" I asked.

"Yes," she said. "Bit rough around the edges, when it comes to apple varieties. Confused a Cortland with a Mac today. But, he'll learn. They always do."

"I can't believe this. *That's* what you're concerned about? He got some variation wrong?" I asked her. I had bigger questions in mind, like: What was he thinking, applying for a job to work here, side by side with *me*? This was my grandparents' store. My home base in Bridgeport, whether I was visiting for a day or a week. Why did he want to be part of it?

Nana looked stunned. "I don't understand. Am I not supposed to care? We tout ourselves as the ones who know apples!"

"Nana, please. I mean, I'm sorry," I said. "This isn't about apples."

"It's not?" she asked. In her mind, everything went back to apples somehow, or at least that's how she made it seem.

"No. It's about you hiring him. You *know* Jackson and I—we aren't—I mean, we don't—I mean, it's weird—I mean, I can't believe—"

"Actually, Luce, I don't know *what* you mean," my grandmother said, taking hold of my shoulders. "What's the problem?"

Oh, nothing. It's just that my very own grandparents betrayed me. "Jackson and I—we have this history," I said. "Not, you know, a very *good* history."

Her eyes widened. "Such as? Lucy, you'd better tell me right now."

"Sorry, it's not that bad." I put my hand on her arm, wanting to put her at ease, even though it *was* pretty awful, from my perspective. "We just—it's awkward between us now. Really, incredibly awkward. I don't want to go into details, but we used to be friends," I said. "Good friends. But we honestly haven't spoken in about three years."

"Well, how were we supposed to know you had a falling-out?" My grandmother sat back down and resumed punching numbers into the adding machine. "His grandparents said he needed a job. He's reliable, a good kid—his references are impeccable. I remembered you used to be friends—seemed like a perfect plan to me."

"When we were little kids, Nana," I said. "Little! Like, tiny!"

"When was that?" she asked.

"Eighth grade," I said. "Okay?"

My grandmother looked up from the adding machine, over her reading glasses, at me. "I hardly think you were a little kid in eighth grade. In fact I distinctly remember you telling me, 'Nana, I'm in eighth grade, you don't need to follow me around the carnival. Nana, I can stay up until midnight, I'm fourteen.'"

"So I wasn't *little* little," I admitted. "That's beside the point, Nana. I was only fourteen."

She gazed at the ceiling and rolled her eyes, like being seventeen was not all that different from being fourteen.

But come on. It *is*. Even *she* knew that, but she was just trying to tease me.

"So you're not close anymore, so what? You don't need to be best buds, you just need to work together. Anyway, you two are practically adults. You'll work it out," she said crisply.

"I doubt it," I said under my breath.

"And Lucy? I don't want to hear any more complaining about it. Jackson's family lives in this town and so do we," Nana said. "One fact you should know about a small town is that sometimes people just have to learn to get along, like it or not."

Not. Very much not. A hundred times not.

"Now, if you don't mind, how about doing some actual work? I've got crates and boxes in the back room I need you to unload."

"I didn't think I was starting today," I said. "I don't have my shirt—"

"Excuses, excuses. We'll get your shirt while we're back there. And are you saying you can't move crates in a tank top?" She smiled and I followed her into the cold storage, rubbing my arms as the chill hit me. I thought about suggesting that the uniforms should be hooded sweatshirts instead of T-shirts.

I decided not to mention it. She was already annoyed with

me and this was only Day One.

Someday she'd understand why seeing Jackson had upset me so much. Maybe not upset me—thrown me for a loop. In fact, the first day Jackson and I worked together, it would be fairly obvious that getting along was pretty much impossible—considering what had happened way back then, not to mention the fact we hadn't talked until a couple of minutes ago, and that was only saying hi.

"Nana, is the schedule posted back here?" I asked.

"No, it's in my office—bulletin board behind my desk. It's also a shared calendar online. Not much to it, though," she said. "Jackson works nine to five; you work ten to six. He gets Wednesdays and Sundays off; you get Sundays and Mondays off. Of course, sometimes that'll change, depending on our schedules."

"Terrific." So we'd only be working together *four* days a week. That was still four too many.

I hefted a wooden crate from the shelf above me. The half bushel of Rome apples nearly fell on my head.

"You need your apple muscles," Nana said. She flexed her biceps. For a sixty-seven-year-old, she was kind of fit. At least as fit as I was, which was beyond embarrassing. Why hadn't she told me that I needed to be in shape for this job? Not that I wasn't in shape . . . for soccer, anyway. Maybe she'd have apples I could kick around at some point.

I slipped my cell phone out of my pocket and glanced at the screen to see if I had any texts from Mikayla about how her check-in was going. I couldn't wait to tell her what had happened and how I'd seen Jackson. She wouldn't totally get it, since I'd met her after the thing with him happened—but she'd definitely be able to commiserate with me. She had a good shoulder to cry on. I'd had to use it before.

"Now, let's get your T-shirt," my grandmother said. "Try this on—it's a small."

As I held up the T-shirt to check whether it would fit, a picture of Jackson in the same exact shirt flashed in my mind. He'd changed so much even since the last time I'd seen him. Of course, the last time I'd seen him I'd crossed the street to avoid him, so I couldn't be sure what had changed about him from year to year. All I knew was, he was tall and his voice had dropped. If I'd gone through that much of a transformation, I certainly didn't *feel* like I had.

As much as I didn't want to admit it, the thing with Jackson had kind of squashed any more risk taking on my part—not just when it came to boys but in other ways, too. I did things when I knew they'd turn out well, for the most part.

But there I was, Day One in Bridgeport. I'd taken a slight,

teensy, tiny risk moving here for the summer instead of staying back home and doing the coffee shop gig again, and look what had happened. It couldn't just go easily, no, of course not. I couldn't work with an old friend like Claire; or some good-looking guy I'd never met; or someone I'd become good friends with, the way I was with Mikayla. No. I was getting Jackson, the boy who'd pretty much humiliated me in eighth grade. I had the worst luck.

"Well, are you going to try it on or not?" my grandmother asked.

"Sure, of course." I walked quickly to the restroom in the back corner of the store and closed the door. I pulled the T-shirt on and looked at myself in the small oval mirror above the sink. Okay, so a few strands of my long, dark brown hair were out of place, a teeny bit of mascara had flaked, and I could use a fresh coat of lip gloss. But at least I hadn't looked completely terrible when I'd run into Jackson.

I made a face at the mirror, scrunching my face up into a frown. The summer wasn't supposed to start like this— at all. I felt like I'd been dribbling the soccer ball down the field effortlessly, making all the right moves, about to score a goal—and someone had just stolen the ball from me, leaving me standing there, looking ridiculous.

I needed to catch my balance and get back on goal—fast.

CHAPTER 4

Mikayla

"That's a sauna?" I asked.

Sarah, the assistant manager at Bridgeport Beach Club, was giving me a tour and a rundown of the Club's policies and procedures. Her friend Henry was tagging along, even though he'd already worked at the Club for a couple of years. The two of them were both in college and home for the summer—Sarah had just finished her sophomore year, while Henry had completed his junior year.

"It is," Sarah told me. "You like saunas?"

"I've never tried one," I said. "Which is kind of why I didn't recognize what it was." I laughed, somewhat nervously. "If you hadn't told me, I'd have guessed it was a coat closet."

"You can wear a coat, but I wouldn't recommend it."

Sarah laughed. "It's, like, a hundred and twenty degrees in there."

"No, thanks," Henry said. "I can't stand anything over eighty."

"Neither can I." Henry and I had already bonded over how hot it had been in Minneapolis the summer before. I had no trouble talking with Henry. He was already spoken for—he'd told me within five minutes of meeting him that he was missing his boyfriend, Charles, who'd gone home to New York for the summer and was working at an art gallery, while Henry had to swap out pool towels.

"Charles and Henry—what are you, both part of the royal family or something?" I teased him.

"No, but we both have complete Anglophile parents," he said.

"So, Mikayla, speaking of, uh, parents," Sarah said. She looked around the lobby where we were standing, as if to make sure no one else was in earshot. The only person I saw was a middle-aged woman covered head to toe in designer sportswear—down to her matching tennis racket cover and sunglasses. "Some of the members here can be a little bit on the snobby side."

"A *little*?" Henry cried. "Some of them think they really *are* royalty. Well, actually, some royals from Norway did stay here last year, so they earned it."

"But the kids—who you'll be spending your days with—are great. If you get a parent who's extremely demanding and not in a nice way? Just buzz me. We all have our own walkie-talkies. And anyway, what are you complaining about?" Sarah asked Henry. "If the people are so difficult, then why do you keep coming back to work here every summer?"

"I like the abuse?" he said.

Sarah laughed and pushed him gently with her hand. "Shut up."

Henry smiled and laughed. "See? I love that. *More*, please." He turned to me. "Also, I can't stand being anywhere truly hot for the summer. Bridgeport can be downright chilly—you know that, right?"

"I've been warned," I said.

"So can I ask you something? What happened to your forehead?" Henry asked.

"I had a little spill on my bike on the way in. Kind of almost ran into a car."

"You ran into a *car*?" Sarah asked. "Are you sure you're all right?"

"It's nothing," I assured her. "So will there be a group orientation I need to attend? Or am I the only new person here this year?" I asked.

"Not all of us have worked here before," Henry said. "But, well, most of us. How did you get in, anyway? Who did you have to bribe to land a job here?"

I laughed. "My friend's grandmother made a call and put in a good word for me. I think that's pretty much it."

"Yeah, connections are everything around here," said Henry. "My grandfather's in charge of deciding who gets a food booth at the Apple Fest every September. It's cutthroat. People offer him actual bribes. Speaking of which, her uncle runs the Walleye Mafia." He pointed to Sarah.

The first time I'd heard about the Walleye Mafia, I pictured gangsters in pinstriped suits hanging out on the docks, shooting up walleye fish with submachine guns, but it's just the name of a popular restaurant in Bridgeport that happens to have the best deck in town. "So do you work there, too?" I asked.

"Been there, done that. I still help out sometimes, but I needed a change," Sarah said. "I'm majoring in event management so I wanted to get a manager position. And my aunt will never budge from *her* job." She smiled. "I worked here part-time last summer, so the managers, Angie and Terry, offered me this position. Anyway, not everyone has a connection somewhere that helps them get a job here, and even people with connections aren't hired automatically. Angie and Terry are picky," said Sarah. "They typically recruit people for their skills, so you must be really good at something."

She was right, but I didn't want to brag. I didn't do that, as a rule. "No, not really," I said.

Sarah folded her arms and looked at me. "Let me guess. You're about five feet nine, and you play basketball, small forward, volleyball—but not beach volleyball, real team volleyball—and you have a killer serve in tennis that you don't usually let people know about until they agree to play a set, and by then it's too late for them to back out."

"Five ten, actually." A small grin spread across my face. "Did you read my job application? I thought that was confidential."

"That's all true?" she said, laughing. "I was mostly just making it up. I think Angie mentioned the volleyball thing, to be honest."

"Everything except tennis. I mean, I can play, but I'm more of a runner," I said.

"Yeah, I can sort of see that in you. So no worries, you'll do great here," Sarah said.

"You weren't actually worried, were you?" asked Henry.

I shook my head. I didn't worry about things like jobs, or sports, or how I'd do at something like this. I was good at lots of things and confident about that. There was just one thing that made me feel completely inept, and that was talking to guys.

Lucy and I were planning to be more outgoing this summer, hoping that it might be easier for us here because we'd have no choice but to get out of our comfort zones. Sure, I could have stayed home in Minneapolis, teaching middle school volleyball and basketball camps during the day and working at the neighborhood Dairy Queen every night I could get a shift. But that was the same old routine.

Plus, we got an entire house to ourselves. Having two younger stepbrothers and one two-year-old half sister, I was used to a more crowded house, and I loved it, in some ways. But I was looking forward to the downtime.

"Okay, back to the tour. And then we'll get your keycard ready and take your photo for the employee list," said Sarah.

"And your fingerprints. She'll need those," Henry said. "Your DNA, your passport . . . they take it all at the BBC." He said *BBC* with an English accent, like he was suddenly covering the royal wedding.

"Come on, let's go outside," said Sarah. "Maybe the fresh air will make Henry stop being so insane."

"Hopeless. I've been trying that for years," Henry said. "Don't you want to show her the secret entrance to the underground bowling alley?"

I stared at him. "Seriously?"

"Ignore him," Sarah said, as Henry disappeared down the hallway with a wave over his shoulder. "Actually, before we head outside, let's pop by the supply room. We still need to get you a couple of uniforms."

The supply "room" was more like a gigantic closet. Shirts and shorts were folded neatly on shelves, below shelves of ball caps, above shelves of sweatshirts and sweatpants. Everything was folded just so. Nothing was out of place.

It kind of reminded me of my dad's closet. He's the most organized person I've ever met. Of course, he kind of has to be, with the amount of space he has and the number of people in our house.

Sarah quickly grabbed a few shirts from each stack and handed them to me. "Take a couple different sizes and try them on later. You never know with this stuff. You can bring back whatever doesn't work."

"Okay," I said slowly, wondering how I was going to carry all of this on my bike as my arms filled with folded shirts, a wind jacket, and a baseball cap.

"I know it's a lot, but trust me," she said. "You'll need multiples. Do you want to wash this stuff every night?"

I shook my head rapidly. Definitely not. "I don't even know if our place has a washer and dryer," I said. "I didn't even look yet! Wow, I really hope so."

"Why? Where are you staying?" Sarah asked.

"I'm living with a friend from home," I said. "We have this kind of rustic cabin—"

"A guy? Are you living with your boyfriend?" she asked excitedly.

"Hardly!" I laughed. "No, it's one of my best friends, Lucy."

"You guys have your own place? Like, totally to yourselves?" Sarah asked.

I nodded. "But it's not in great shape. I mean, it's got some chipped paint, missing shingles, and barely a stick of furniture. You should see the place."

"Who cares what condition it's in?" Sarah said. "You can fix it up, right? I'm so jealous that you're living on your own. You could be living under a tent and I'd be jealous. I'll have to come by and check it out sometime."

"Oh, definitely," I said. "But don't expect much."

Sarah laughed. "So you guys planning some parties, or what? I know that's what I would do if I had my own house this summer. I'd invite half the town."

"Maybe you could help us plan it, then?" I smiled, picturing the event Sarah might have in mind versus our ramshackle cabin, which would probably only hold about twenty or twenty-five people comfortably—and that was with everyone standing. Then again, it was summer; no need to stay indoors. And Lucy and I were committed to breaking out of our shells. Not that many people knew us here; we could be whoever and whatever we wanted to be. That was the whole point of going somewhere new for a while: to start over, to reboot.

I pictured our living room, kitchen, and deck crowded with people on a Saturday night. It could actually happen.

CHAPTER 5

Lucy

"Where is this yard sale? Shouldn't we be there by now?" I asked.

Mikayla scanned her phone with her pinky finger. "According to this . . . we should be turning right up here."

I came to a stop sign. We could either go straight, or turn left. "There's no right. Should I go left?" I asked.

"Maybe I have this upside down," Mikayla wondered out loud. She stared at her phone, then rotated it a hundred and eighty degrees.

I pulled over to the side of the road so I could look at the map. Not that I had a great, or even all that good, sense of direction, but couldn't a map app help us with that? I studied the pin that showed our location.

"We've gone too far," I said. "We need to turn around."

"Us, going too far? That's a first," Mikayla joked.

"Ha ha," I said in a monotone. Then I cracked up laughing, because it was all too true.

We'd been in our little cabin for one night and were already out the next morning looking for things to add to it. We needed groceries for the fridge, some more towels, curtains, a bath mat, a rug for the entryway—in fact, we were going to go into debt before we both started working on Thursday and got our first paychecks a week later.

I'd scanned a local website looking for garage sales and yard sales: most were on the weekend, but a few started today.

"I wish we were at home. I'd know exactly where to go thrifting for furniture," Mikayla said. "Do you think it's too late to make a quick road trip?"

"It might be quicker than us trying to find Sandstone Road," I muttered, staring at the map. Suddenly I noticed a landmark I recognized. "Now I know where we are. We have to turn around."

We drove back toward town and made a few turns, before ending up at the house having a yard sale. It looked a little run-down, but then again, so did our summerhouse. "This looks like one of those reality shows my mom loves, where we're going to find some incredibly valuable item for a dollar.

Then we sell it at auction and become filthy rich."

"I wish," said Mikayla as we climbed out of the car. "Then we could use the money to pay for college."

"Or a trip around the world," I said. "I mean, come on. Let's think of something more exciting."

"Hey, funding college might not be thrilling, but it's practical. If Ava got that kind of money, she'd probably blow it all on shoes," Mikayla said, laughing. "Like last fall when she spent three hundred dollars on that pair she wore to homecoming—one night. Three hundred dollars."

"Yeah, and remember how her mom forced her to take them back the next day, after she'd danced in them all night?" I said.

But somehow she got away with it. Ava had a knack for pulling off things that nobody else would be able to.

I'd only been friends with Ava and Mikayla since ninth grade, when my parents decided to send me to a private high school. Oak Hills Academy (we called it OH! for short) had an insane dose of math, science, and classics, and a killer arts program. The three of us met during freshman orientation, a daylong event where we were broken into small groups called "pods" to get to know each other. Our group was called the Turtle Pod. We totally resented that. We're not slow. We wanted to be in the Fox Pod, the Tiger Pod . . . something a little more sexy. "Turtles," Ava had said at the time. "We're the only ones named after reptiles. What, were snakes already taken?"

We bonded when we had to carry an egg in a spoon across the football field. "We should be good at this," Mikayla said. "Turtles carry eggs all the time."

We were doing okay until Mikayla tried to go too fast, and the egg went flying, hit me on the ear, and smashed. We couldn't stop laughing. As disgusting as it felt to have egg white dripping down my face, it was funny. Ava came to the rescue with Kleenex to clean me up, and she's kind of been coming to our rescue ever since.

When school started, the three of us didn't have many activities in common: Mikayla played fall volleyball while I was on the soccer team, and Ava tried one thing, then another. But the three of us had some classes together, and that was enough to keep forming a bond. I helped Mikayla and Ava get through biology, geometry, and pre-chemistry; Mikayla helped me and Ava get through US history and world history; and Ava helped us loosen up and have fun when we got too serious and studied too much. She was also a good writer, and had published poems in our school literary magazine.

We never had to go through orientation again, but we still teamed up for other major school events. Sophomore year we'd raised hundreds of dollars for the school travel club by selling concessions in the hallways at lunch—Ava would walk around yelling "Everything's a dollar!" into a bullhorn while Mikayla and I carried the cookies, trail mix, fruit, and other items Ava got her mom to buy in bulk. "We're like a walking Costco. You guys realize that," Mikayla had said at one point. "And, like Costco, we have tons of returning customers," Ava would say. Basically, she did all the talking and selling. Mikayla and I just handed stuff over and took the money.

We were hoping we'd make enough to go to France, but instead we ended up on buses to Washington, DC, which was one of the most fun trips I've ever taken. The three of us shared a room and stayed up later and later every night until we collapsed on the charter bus five days later and slept almost all the way back to Minnesota.

Now, Mikayla and I kept wandering around the yard sale, examining china, candlesticks, a couple of dated avocado-colored chairs with cigarette burns—and matching avocado ashtrays. Then we saw exactly what we were looking for: a retro kitchen table with four chairs. Unfortunately, it was $300.

We ended up finding a folding table and chairs for fifty dollars.

We were trying to fit everything into the back of the car

when I heard a loud honk. The car honked again. I looked behind me and saw Claire parking right in back of us. I'd texted her that morning, asking for clues on where to find something.

"You guys need help?" she asked, coming up to the car. "What did you buy, anyway?"

"It's the chairs. They don't fold down small enough," I said, laughing. "Claire, this is Mikayla, and vice versa."

"Hey, Claire. I've heard so much about you. I think the one time I came to visit, you were gone," Mikayla said.

"Really? But I feel like I never leave." Claire laughed.

She helped us get the furniture squarely into the car. On the edge of the parking lot, a few younger kids had set up a lemonade and cookie stand. We walked over to buy a few cups.

"To summer!" I said, tapping my cup against Mikayla's.

"To summer!" she agreed.

"Ditto," said Claire, hoisting her plastic cup in the air.

I took a gulp of the cold lemonade.

It tasted like sour lemon meringue pie—it was too thick, and seemed to have no sugar. We all spit it out onto the black-top, laughing. "So much for toasts," I said.

Mikayla crumpled her cup. "We should have known bet-ter. We should have toasted with a cookie."

CHAPTER 6

Mikayla

"Have you heard from Ava yet?" I asked, as Lucy and I walked past Walleye Mafia on Wednesday night. The name was written on a large fish-shaped wooden sign hanging over the front door. The fish had a spaghetti pattern carved on its side and pepperoni-like red circles for eyes.

"No. I keep checking, but there's nothing. Instead, I have about eighty-seven texts from my mom," Lucy said. "And I've only been gone for two days."

"Did you expect anything different?" I asked. Lucy's mom was notorious for being in touch with her—or trying to be—at all times of the day and night. She even texted her at home, when they were in the same house. I skimmed my messages again. "I haven't heard from Ava either. That's weird, don't you think? I wonder if she's okay."

"She's probably so busy—she's forgotten us already. Living the high life in Chicago," said Lucy.

"What's the high life?"

"I don't know, it's something my mom always says. Help me. I'm quoting my mom." Lucy laughed. "Maybe Ava burned through her phone plan. Ever since the famous Sophomore Year Overage Incident she's been paying for it herself and—" Suddenly Lucy grabbed my arm. "Wait. What if we run into Jackson here?" Lucy was scoping out Earl Grey's from the entrance. She looked nervous.

We were poised on the doorstep, halfway in and halfway out. I felt really self-conscious standing there. A couple had to squeeze to get past us. "I don't know. What are the odds he'd walk in right now? Pretty slim, right?" I asked. I had to flatten my back against the community bulletin board to make room for some other people leaving. I felt like I was being tortured by pins. And ads for rooms to rent.

"I'm trying to think. I guess I came here last summer and I don't remember seeing him here, so maybe he doesn't hang out, or maybe he doesn't like tea. Or maybe I've just been incredibly lucky so far. . . ." She was standing on her tiptoes peering around the coffee shop.

"Um, Luce? You can't spend the whole summer trying to

avoid him," I said. "It's going to be impossible. You'll waste way too much time and energy trying."

"Good point," Lucy said. "But I still want to."

"Besides, you can't avoid him at work, so you're going to have to get used to seeing him and talking to him, like it or not. I wouldn't spend your time worrying about it." I pushed her forward into the shop, toward the line, so we could actually order.

"Why do you have to be so grown-up and mature sounding?" Lucy complained. She ordered an iced tea and I opted for a hot chai latte. Once we got our drinks, we moved into the far room and found a table to sit at, near the small wooden stage where musicians performed on the weekends. I remembered coming to a couple of shows the summer before.

"Luce, you're fine. That was so long ago. You're different."

"I don't feel all that different," Lucy said. "I know I should, but it's still so embarrassing. And then beyond that, it just really sucked to lose a friend."

"So how would I recognize Jackson if I did see him?" I asked. "I still don't even know what he looks like, remember?"

"You know, I don't have any pictures of him, and even if I did he wouldn't look the same now," Lucy said.

"Facebook?" I suggested.

"Even easier, you can see him at the store, I guess." Lucy

put her head in her hands. "The store. I can't believe we're working together at the store. I mean, just shoot me now."

"Maybe you won't work together that often. You won't have the same shifts all the time, right?" I asked. "There will be other people working there to make it easier."

"There are only the two of us, remember? The store isn't that big. And my grandparents don't trust anyone else," Lucy said.

"How about if you ask your grandmother to cut back on his hours?" I suggested.

"Ha! I can't ask my grandmother to do anything," she said. "I told her that it might be extremely awkward and she wasn't sympathetic at all. She said I'd just have to get over it. And she's right. I mean, we're *going* to have this totally awesome summer—I won't let the fact that Jackson's my coworker ruin it for me." She paused. "I guess I knew he could be around, since his grandparents live here too, but I didn't consider that—you know."

"You'd be coworkers," I said.

"Exactly." She sipped her iced tea. "Okay, so tell me about some of *your* coworkers for a change. There has to be more than one. Any cute guys?"

I thought back to my first day at the Club. "There's this guy at the security gate named Liam. He's slightly rude." I touched my forehead gingerly to see how my cut was doing. "And I nearly ran into someone on my bike. He was attractive but I'm sure he was on his way out of town, because that would be my luck."

Lucy didn't respond at first—she didn't even seem to be listening to me. She was staring across the room, or maybe into space. "I just thought of something," she said.

"What?" I asked.

"Could *I* get a job at the Club?" she said, sounding excited by the prospect. "Because that would solve a lot of my problems. I mean, my main problem. Jackson," she said in a soft voice, as if I didn't know what or who she was talking about.

"Do you seriously think your grandparents would be okay with you working somewhere else? You're their apple star," I reminded her.

"Apple ambassador," she corrected me.

I rolled my eyes. "Whatever."

"No, probably not. Nana pleaded with me for months and got us the house. I can't ditch her now." Lucy finished off her iced tea. "I'm going for a refill. You need one?"

"Not yet. I'll hold the table," I said. The place was filling up fast. I picked up a discarded local free paper from the next table over and started leafing through it, looking for upcoming events. There were free concerts at the pavilion by the main beach, starting that weekend. The deck at Walleye Mafia was hosting live music every Thursday night. Ads for kayak rentals caught my eye; I was hoping to do some exploring by boat over the summer, maybe even an overnight trip by kayak. I was hoping Lucy would feel like adventuring with me, because I wasn't sure I knew enough about the outdoors to pull it off on my own. *Maybe I could find a group to go with*, I mused. The BBC was full of potential friends; I just had to sort out who was who.

I glanced up, wondering what was taking Lucy so long. She was chatting with a couple of girls at a table by the front door—old friends, I guessed, from other summers here.

"Excuse me," a deep voice above me said.

I turned and saw a guy standing in front of me. He looked like he was about my age, or maybe older, in college, because he was wearing a maroon University of Minnesota wrestling T-shirt. (I know. I'm really good at picking up clues about guys that way.) (Eye roll.)

"Hey," he said. "Anyone else have this table?" He gestured to the table next to ours, which still had a coffee mug on it.

"I don't . . . no," I said, shaking my head. "I haven't seen anyone."

"Cool." He brought the mug to the dirty dishes bin, then sat down and scooted in his chair, which was right next to mine. "So, you find anything good in there?" he asked.

"Good?" I said.

"The newspaper?" He pointed at it.

Duh. It was only right in front of my face.

"Should I . . . maybe? I'll check?" Great. Only managed to say, like, two words and I sounded like I had never had a conversation in my life. Was there a school for this? A medication, maybe?

"I was hoping there'd be a show here tonight, but I guess there isn't one. Maybe a local band's playing somewhere else?"

"Uh, I'm not . . . sure. You want?" I held the newspaper to him.

He narrowed his eyes at me. "Where are you from?" he asked.

"Minneapolis?" I said.

He gave me the oddest look, took the paper, pushed his chair back, and walked out of the café. *Whatever*, I thought. Did he have something against Minneapolis? If he just wanted the free newspaper, why didn't he ask for it? Why did he make me have such an awkward conversation? There were free newspapers in a rack by the entrance. What was his problem?

Lucy returned just then, carrying a large cookie along with her refill. "Were you just talking to that guy?"

"No. Not really." Some things were too humiliating to admit even to a close friend.

"Potential?" Lucy asked.

I thought of the look on his face whenever I answered his questions. He probably thought I was from Russia. I did sound a little like my grandmother, who had emigrated to the United States when she was a teenager and still had an accent. She could speak English perfectly, but sometimes she pretended not to when she didn't want to talk to someone—like if someone at the mall asked her to take a survey, or someone outside Bread & Chocolate asked her to sign a petition (some group staked out that corner every weekend). She would say something like "Excusing me, I not understand," and move on.

She would say, "I'm not sure, you want?" and that would be on purpose. I was saying it because I had no "talk to cute boy" function. My model was lacking that. I needed an upgrade.

"But you know what? Maybe it's time we go out on a limb and try to meet someone—talk to someone completely out of the blue, just like he did," I said. "If other people can do it, why can't we?"

"Um, because we're horrible at it?" she reminded me.

I looked around the crowded café. So much potential. So little nerve.

CHAPTER 7

Lucy

You can do this, I told myself on Thursday morning as I walked from the car to The Original Apple Store.

Maybe your history with Jackson says otherwise, but you can do this.

He's just a person. A person who happens to be the reason you wanted to hide under a rock during your eighth-grade graduation ceremony, and the reason all your pictures from that time show a very sad and awkward-looking Lucy. But still, he's just another human being, even if he did act like a horrible one, once upon a time.

I unlocked the door and walked into the Apple Store. My grandfather was standing by the register. Next to him was Jackson.

My pulse was climbing, but not out of control. Probably the apple-scented reed diffusers were having a calming effect on me, the way certain herbal smells are used to calm pets before they get stuck in a kennel and flown cross-country in the cargo hold. We did that for our dog once. Sigh. I missed Kingsley. He lived with my dad now.

We didn't open for customers for another fifteen minutes, so this was our chance to learn anything we hadn't already picked up. Like: how to be around each other after three years of deliberately avoiding each other.

"Good morning, Lucy!" my grandfather's cheerful voice rang out.

"Hi, Grandpa." I gave a little wave and quickly scooted behind the two of them to stash my bag in the little office, up high on a shelf. *Don't sweat it. You can do this*, I told myself as I emerged from the office, taking a deep breath and letting it out the way my mom does in her yoga workouts.

My mantra was starting to bore me. Just because it worked for taking standardized tests didn't mean it would work with people. Besides, who even knew if I could do this? That's the problem with mantras and other things I try to tell myself: they don't always convince me.

When I turned around, Grandpa and Jackson were both

looking at me, as if they were just waiting for me, frozen in time, before they could do another thing.

"Hey," Jackson said. He paused. "Lucy."

Again with greeting me with the long break between words. Well, two could play at that game, even if it was a very dull game. "Hey," I said. Wait for it, wait for it . . . "Jackson."

Only my mouth was all tense because my jaw was clenched so it came out as "Shee-shaw." Like I'd just gotten my jaw wired shut and was only allowed to drink my meals in liquid form.

"About time you showed up, Lucy," Grandpa said.

"What?" It was nine forty-five, which was when they'd told me to be there. I glanced at Jackson. "But you said—"

Grandpa smiled and clapped me on the back. "Just messing with you," he said. "You're right on time."

"Ha ha," I said, pushing him slightly with my shoulder.

"It's just that Jackson here was early, which kind of puts him on the nice list," Grandpa said. "You, on the other hand? Naughty list all the way."

"Grandpa, seriously? Are you really keeping track of that stuff now? Christmas is six months off."

"No kidding. And I'm not Santa Claus—although I did play him once or twice," my grandpa said.

"On TV?" asked Jackson.

"No. In the living room." My grandfather laughed.

I couldn't help noticing that Jackson and I looked kind of idiotic standing there in our Apple Store T-shirts. Like we were siblings and had matching red shirts because it was time for our yearly Christmas picture.

My grandpa and his reference to nice and naughty lists had started me off on a weird train of thought.

Jackson sort of turned toward me, and I panicked, not sure what to do or say. I hurried over to my grandpa as he headed for the back door. "You're going to leave right away? Really?"

"Yes, really," he said.

"But it's our first day! We might need you," I said. *Me in particular. Because I need a buffer between me and Jackson at all times, thank you.*

"The store has a phone. I have a phone. I don't see a problem," he replied. "Besides, your grandmother will be in later."

"Yeah, but . . ."

"Lucy." He smiled. "Did you think we hired you so we could hang out and visit all day? We have things to do. That's why we want you and Jackson to mind the store."

Ouch. "Okay," I said. "No, you're right. Of course. Uh, bye!"

He walked out and I turned around, feeling dumb.

Fortunately, Jackson was busy restocking the apple bar. If he was embarrassed for me for acting like a six-year-old, at least he didn't show it. While his back was turned, I checked him out for a second. How tall exactly had he gotten? Six feet? And me, I had only grown like two inches. How was that fair?

He suddenly turned slightly and I quickly made myself busy straightening a table of T-shirts. Being a weekday early in the season, I didn't really expect the store would get a ton of business. That was a good thing and a bad thing. We needed the time to learn what we were doing, but we might be stuck alone in the store with nothing to say to each other. For eight hours. Eight long, endless, awkward hours.

I got a lunch break, right? I was dying to know if, and when, I got a lunch break. But that would leave Jackson in the store all by himself. That wouldn't be fair. Why had my grandparents not gone over this with us? At my other job, at the coffee chain in the mall, this kind of stuff was set in stone. You couldn't walk a foot without hitting some kind of posted rule, regulation, or encouraging team language.

"So. You do this last summer too?" Jackson asked.

"Oh. No. Uh-uh." I shook my head. "I was in the Cities."

"Really? I could have sworn I saw you up here," he said.

"Maybe on vacation," I said. "I was here for a week or two."

"Oh." He nodded. "I was here the whole summer, so."

"So, yeah." I nodded and sort of laughed. I sounded strange and uncomfortable, which was exactly how I felt. "Um, so did my grandfather go over what we should do?"

"There's a list." Jackson pointed to the counter, near the cash register.

"Right, right." My grandmother had already shown me the list, but I'd forgotten.

I walked over to the counter and found the handwritten, laminated "Daily To-Do" list, with a Post-it note on top saying:

Jackson and Lucy—Here are some ideas for when it's slow. Please make sure to do everything on this list at least once a day—some items are starred and must be done frequently, as needed.

Restock apple bar and rearrange for best visual effect.

Memorize the best uses for each variety of apple; customers will ask.

Clean front doors and window with glass cleaner.

Tidy all folded items: T-shirts, dish towels, fleece, sweatshirts, socks, hats, etc. Refold as needed.

Dust glass countertops and displays.

While I was reading it, Jackson came over to stand beside me. "So what else is on the list? I restocked the apples."

"Um, you want to clean the windows and doors or fold stuff?" I asked.

"Windows and doors," Jackson said.

"Great. Sounds great." While Jackson fetched the bottle of glass cleaner and a roll of paper towels from the utility closet, I started straightening and tidying all the shelves of T-shirts, sweatshirts, towels, dish towels . . . you name it, my grandparents' store stocked it. I have to give them credit, though. Most of what they had wasn't tacky, as far as those things go. Some of it was even cute.

But after a while, it got tedious. I walked over to the front doors to get some fresh air. I fiddled with the iPod they used to play music in the store. I read a few entries in *An Apple Farmer's Almanac*.

"Plant a seed today and feed the world tomorrow."

"North wind at night, grower's delight."

"A bee on the tree is worth two in the hive."

I put the book back on the shelf and glanced at my watch, wondering if it was time for lunch yet. It was only ten forty-five. The days were going to crawl if I didn't talk to Jackson. Besides, I wanted him to know that I was completely cool now—as in, no longer interested in him. At all. The easiest way to do that would be to joke around and show him I wanted only to be a friendly coworker. It didn't mean that I'd forgiven him yet; just that I could see the wisdom of talking to him, if it helped pass the time. Maybe he could even apologize. That could be a conversation.

I migrated to the magnet tree, which was literally a metal tree covered in cute magnets. I absentmindedly ran the feather duster around the tree, stopping when my eye caught a rectangular magnet styled like a book cover: *50 Shades of Apple*. I laughed, wondering if my grandparents even knew what it meant.

I picked up the one that said *The Original Apple Store: iApple—Do You?* and brought it over to show Jackson. "How long before my grandparents get sued for this, do you think?"

He turned to me just as he was spraying the door. The bottle kept spraying and blue window cleaner went right into my eyes.

"Ack!" I cried.

"Sorry!" Jackson said. "You okay?"

Sorry? My eyes were burning and I could hardly see. I was going blind from glass spray. And all he could say was "Sorry"! I rushed to the big sink in the cold storage room and splashed my face with water. My eyes were still burning, so I doused them about a hundred times.

Finally the feeling started to go away. I grabbed a paper towel from the dispenser on the wall to dry my face. I blinked a few times.

"I'm really sorry about that," Jackson said from the doorway. "Are you okay?"

I could still see. Unfortunately. My reflection in the paper towel dispenser was blurry but showed me two things: one, my eye makeup was smudged and disastrous-looking; and two, the neck of my T-shirt was soaked. Great. So this was how I had to start my first day on the job. I dabbed at my eyes, trying to fix the smeared mascara. "I'm fine. Maybe a little drenched, and I might need glasses to see from now on—"

"You can't see?" Jackson asked. "Are you serious? Crap! Where's the phone?"

"Don't ask me! I'm practically blind here," I said.

"No. Come on. Really? I'm so sorry, I—"

I started laughing, despite the stinging pain in my eyes. "Relax. I'm fine."

"You're—you're fine?"

"Really. I was pulling your leg. Kind of," I admitted. It felt good to hear him freak out. Not that I'd be plotting revenge all summer, but seeing him so defensive and apologetic made things a teeny bit better.

"Well, be serious. Is there anything I can do?" Jackson asked. "You need more paper towels?"

"No, I'm good. I'm going to blink a lot for the next couple of hours, but I'll be okay, I think," I said.

"People are going to wonder why you're making faces at them. I can't believe you just did that to me," he said. "I thought I blinded you for life or something."

"I can't believe you just sprayed glass cleaner in my face," I said.

All of a sudden it felt like we were kids again, having a typical argument. We both laughed, breaking some of the tension. Actually, I don't even know how much tension he'd been feeling; but I'd felt pretty crushed by the weight of it.

The phone rang, and Jackson headed to the counter to grab it, while I ducked into the bathroom to see if I could fix my makeup—not that I had any with me, because it was all in my bag in the office. I could just run and grab it, but I wasn't thrilled about looking like a raccoon in public—a sad, tearful raccoon. I was about to dab my eyes with a tissue when there was a gentle knock on the door. "Um, telephone call. For you," Jackson said awkwardly.

"Who is it?" I asked.

"I don't know," he said. "A girl's voice?"

I quickly swiped the tissue across my face and tossed it into the trash can. When I walked back out, the store had suddenly filled with customers. "What's going on? Bus tour?" I asked Jackson as I hurried to the phone, on the wall by the register. I'd have to get rid of whoever it was—probably Mikayla. I hoped her first day at work wasn't going as badly as mine was.

"Lucyloo! It's Mom. You didn't answer your phone, and I got worried so I called the store."

"Mom. The reason I didn't answer is because I'm at work. At the store," I explained. I'd just talked to her an hour or so ago when she called to check in, and told her that I was on my way.

"Well, anyway, have you found a good dress yet? Because I'm standing here at this new shop on Fiftieth and France, and they have the cutest—"

"Mom. Mom! I can't talk right now. I'm at work," I said. Again.

My parents had been divorced for a little over two years, and now both were engaged and planning on getting remarried soon, maybe even during the summer. I couldn't believe how quickly they'd moved on, especially considering they'd been married for fifteen years.

I knew that if I'd stayed at home for the summer, I'd be buried in wedding plans, helping my mother with every detail and doing a thousand errands for her. That didn't mean she wouldn't drag me in as much as she could over the phone.

My dad and his fiancée were planning a small wedding in the fall, and they'd asked me to do a reading for the ceremony—in addition to being a bridesmaid—so I'd been leafing through my giant poetry anthology from school, searching for a good passage. My dad's wedding would be much more low-key than my mom's. I was counting on it, in fact.

"But this dress is perfect for you. I can just see it with a nice pair of earrings and then some sandals . . ."

I suddenly caught my reflection in the small apple-shaped mirror on the wall beside the phone. I no longer had raccoon eyes. Now I looked like a goth clown. I grabbed my purse from the office shelf, found a tube of lip balm, and started using it as a makeup remover. "Mom, please, I have to get back to work. I'll call you later," I said.

"Oh, look at that necklace. I might need that. Anyway, let me describe this dress to you. It's sort of a peach. Would you say it's peach or more poppy?" she started asking someone at the store.

"No—don't!" I said. I had visions of spending my entire summer on the phone with my mom. With the wedding planning going on, she'd probably be calling me thirty times more than she usually did. "I need to wait on some customers."

"But I need to know now. I also need help with the cake, and the decorations, but we can talk about that later. So what about this dress?" she asked. "Should I pick it up while I'm here?"

"Your call. Gotta go, Mom. Love you." I hung up the red phone on the wall. Was she going to call me every day at work? I could just see her doing that. When I went to a week-long soccer camp in tenth grade, she was famous for calling me every other hour to make sure I was drinking enough water—and to tell me what she'd been doing in the time since we last spoke.

As I walked back out to the register, I saw a line of about five people waiting. Had I been on the phone *that* long?

"How do you ring these up?" Jackson said, showing me a

handful of red candles.

"Carefully?" I said, stepping up beside him.

He handed them to me. His hand was sort of shaking, and the candles felt a little mushy. He was nervous. That made me smile. Good. I wasn't the only nervous wreck around here. Just the one who knew how to ring up teeny little apple-shaped votive candles that were practically melting. But was he nervous because of me and our awkward past, or because he didn't know they were three for five dollars?

"You ring, I'll bag," he said. "I'm good at that, anyway. Two years working after school at Lunds," he added, referring to a grocery store back home. He shook out a small red handled bag and started filling it with Original Apple Store goods.

As I turned to swipe the credit card, we bumped elbows. I'm pretty sure it was the closest we'd stood to each other in three years. Since that disastrous day at the pool. I kind of hoped he didn't remember that as well as I did.

CHAPTER 8

Mikayla

"Where's your swimsuit?" Sarah asked, walking up beside me as I stood near the lake. Having just figured out how to keep ten kids from killing each other with tennis rackets for the past couple of hours, I was ready for a break. I slipped off my Nikes and walked onto the warm sand.

"I didn't bring it," I replied. "Why?"

My body was exhausted. I felt like I'd just run a marathon—not that I've done a real marathon . . . yet. But I think training for one could be easier than getting five- and six-year-olds to understand why zero was called *love* and why scores went up by fifteen and then by ten.

"Aw, you should have. Go buy one in the gift shop," Henry

said, following closely behind her. If Sarah was the assistant manager, then Henry was the assistant manager's assistant. They seemed to go everywhere together.

"They don't sell swimsuits in the gift shop," Sarah said. "They sell *robes*. White terrycloth robes with the BBC logo."

"Oh. Well, swimming in a robe could be interesting," Henry said. "You'd look slightly insane, like you just escaped the asylum, but at least you'd be covered up."

"What asylum? And somehow, I don't think that would work." I glanced down at my clothes. I was wearing a polo shirt and shorts—my official BBC uniform. Well, at least it was one of many. It wouldn't matter if I got the clothes wet—I had another set just waiting for me at home.

I emptied my pockets and slid my jewelry into the toe of my tennis shoes. "Last one in is a rotten egg!" I yelled, then took off sprinting for the water, my feet tossing up sand behind me.

"You're kidding, right?" Sarah called as she ran after me.

"I hate eggs!" Henry yelled, following close behind. "I'm ovo-intolerant!"

"Ovo-what?" I yelled back over my shoulder, then I plunged into the lake. The bracing jolt of ice-cold water took my breath away.

Oh no, oh no. How could I have forgotten how flipping

cold the lake was? This was June, early in the season, and this was northern Minnesota, not Mexico. I was an idiot.

But at least I had company. "This lake is f-f-freezing!" I said, my teeth chattering.

"Keep swimming," Henry said, his arms slicing through the water beside me. "Until hypothermia sets in, then get out if you can still move."

Sarah was swimming on her back, kicking spray into the air. "Isn't this why we have two heated pools? So we don't have to do this?"

After another minute we raced just as quickly out of the water as we had into it. Elizabeth, who worked in the membership office, was waiting on the shore with a stack of white towels. She tossed one to each of us. "You guys are insane. You know that, right?"

"Oh, thank you," I said, wrapping the towel around my shoulders. Standing around in a wet shirt wasn't my idea of fun.

"We're going for the record this year," said Sarah. "We're going in every single Friday. Right, Mikayla?"

"We are?" I asked. "First I've heard of it."

"Come on, it'll be fun," Sarah said. "I'll make up some kind of award."

"Well, maybe if I bring my suit next Friday. That would

help." I clutched the towel tighter around my shoulders.

"Get dried off and come with us to Earl Grey's," Henry said. "A bunch of us are going—you can meet everyone and learn all the dirt."

"Everyone who?" I said. "And what dirt?"

"I can't tell you *now*," Henry said. "Then you wouldn't show up."

"Of course I'll show up. What time?" I asked.

"You know where Grey's is?" Sarah asked, and I nodded. "Be there at six thirty."

I finished toweling off, got my jewelry and slipped everything back on, and put my coins back in my pocket, along with a short pencil I'd been using to keep score in Yahtzee with a group of very competitive kids. I went inside to grab my backpack and helmet, then headed to my bike, waving to a bunch of people along the way. I was really starting to feel at home at the BBC—at least, with my coworkers. It was like an instant group of friends.

"Hey, Mikayla!" Sarah called after me. "You want a ride tonight? I can pick you up."

"Uh, sure," I said. "That would be great!" I walked over to quickly give her directions to the cabin on Hemlock Hill Road. It was fairly easy to find—as long as you weren't looking for much of an actual *house*.

❖❖❖

I quickly checked in with Lucy to see if she wanted to come along, but she was headed to her grandparents' house for dinner right after work. I tried to convince her to meet me a little bit later, but she had plans with Claire for *after* dinner. So I took a quick shower and changed into jeans and a couple of layering T-shirts. I spent time blow-drying my hair and dabbed some makeup on the last remaining scratch on my face.

I heard Sarah's car pull into the gravel driveway and went out to meet her, so she'd know she was at the right address.

"Huh," she said as she climbed out of the car and examined the house.

"That's kind of how I felt the first time I saw it," I admitted. "But it's really not bad. Just slightly in the woods."

"Woods are cool," she said. "Woods have charm."

The screen door nearly fell off its hinges when I opened it wide to let her into the cabin. "Don't speak too soon," I said, laughing.

"Wow. How old *is* this place?" she asked as we walked inside.

"I'm not sure. It needs some work—no one's lived here for a while, and it had that abandoned look when we arrived. We're doing extra painting to give it some color, Lucy's grandfather has fixed a few things, and we're gradually getting some furniture."

"It just needs a little TLC, that's all." Sarah walked through the cottage to the large deck on the back side. "This is so nice and secluded. Oh, and you can kind of see the islands. Sweet!"

I nodded. "It's one of the perks, for sure."

"I would *not* have expected that. People are going to love hanging out here. That is, if you have a party. I seriously don't mean to pressure you about it," she said with a laugh.

"No, it's exactly what we've been thinking too!" Wasn't one of the whole points of the summer to have fun and meet new people—and possibly have a whirlwind romance?

Ha. Whirlwind. My previous efforts were more like slight breezes.

There was the time I ran into Brandon W., my fall crush, in the school parking lot and said, "Um . . . it smells like tar, doesn't it?" He said nothing in reply. Shocking.

Then in the spring, I decided I'd turn over a new leaf and talk to Quinn M., my spring crush, while we were both waiting for the bus to our track meet. He asked what events I was in, and I said, "The fifteenhurdlehundredhigh." And he said, "Good luck," and sat somewhere else, anywhere else, far, far away from me.

"I'll talk to Lucy about when a good day for a party might be," I said. "But we'll need you to help spread the word about it, since we don't know that many people here yet. Sound good?"

"Definitely," Sarah said. "You ready to start meeting more people?"

"Sure." I smiled nervously as we headed outside to her car. What was the worst that could happen?

Earl Grey's seemed especially packed when we arrived, but I guess I shouldn't have been surprised, since it was Saturday night.

Henry and his friends had claimed a big round table in the back, but it was already filled by so many people that I wondered if there would be room for us to join them.

Then I got closer and realized that the guy I'd nearly plowed into on my bike a week ago was at the table too. *Wait a second. They know him?*

My first instinct was to run and hide. *You can't leave*, I reminded myself. *One, it'll look dumb, and two, you don't have a ride home.*

Well, there was always jogging, but . . . I glanced down at my sandals. Not in these shoes.

So I borrowed a chair from another table and pulled it

over to squeeze into a tiny space next to Sarah, who'd taken the last open chair at the table.

"It's her." Henry pointed at me with a straw when I sat down.

"It's me . . . what?" I asked.

"*She* totally took your job, didn't she?" Henry asked the boy I'd nearly crashed into on my bike.

"What? No." He laughed. "It's my fault I'm not working at the Club this summer. They gave up my spot because I told them to."

"To *me*?" I said, flustered. "I'm sorry. Do you . . . want it back?" I lifted my hands in some sort of awkward gesture. Like I could actually give it back, as if it were a thing.

"Of course not. Don't sweat it," he said, glancing at me. If he recognized me from the day we met, he didn't show it. Was that why he'd nearly run me down? I was a job thief? "I didn't know I would be around here until it was too late. I was going to spend the summer in the Cities," he said.

He lived in the Cities—like me. But which one? This was key. Don't ask me why, it just was. *Go ahead,* I said to myself. *Ask him where he lives. At the very least get his name so you can look him up online.*

"My uncle has a landscaping business and always needs help. Or he *said* he did, until he realized he didn't," he explained. "I was so mad. So was my mom; they're barely speaking right now. Anyway, by then, the Club was full up, so I got a couple of different jobs. It's fine, I'm going to make a decent amount of money either way."

"Well, good," I said. "I'd feel horrible if I was the reason you were out of work."

"Don't listen to anything Henry says. That's the first rule of working at the Club," he advised me.

"Yeah. I kind of figured that out on Day One when he told me about the underground bowling alley," I said, rolling my eyes.

"I resent that," Henry said. "And it's the BBC, not Club."

"Whatever," Sarah said. "You want to pretend you're working in London, go right ahead. But I don't think you'd see this many North Shore T-shirts there."

Everyone started in with examples of how Bridgeport was nothing like London, and I decided to go get something to drink, grabbing Sarah's order as well. I had just joined the line when Bike Crash Guy came up to stand behind me. "You might have taken my job, but I almost ran you over, so we're probably even," he said.

"You remember that?" I asked.

"Why would I not remember that?" he said. "It only

happened a few days ago."

"Monday," I said. Not that I'd been keeping track or anything.

"Monday, right," he said. "Doesn't seem like that long since I saw you. Of course, you had a bike helmet on, and your forehead was bleeding—"

"It was not that bad," I said, laughing. "Well, except for the gash on my leg." I showed him the wound that still remained, a jagged scab about four inches long. *Wait a second. Did I just tell him to look at my leg?* He was definitely checking it out, which was really awkward. "Hey, I didn't—did I really take your job?" I asked, trying to change the focus.

"No, I was just joking. I don't mind." He shrugged, then looked at me more carefully. "I can tell you don't believe me. I'm being serious!"

"Okay, I believe you. I guess." I ordered a cold press from the barista, and took a deep breath before I turned back around to face him. This was going kind of okay so far. I didn't know whether to be stunned, or impressed with myself.

He ordered an Arnold Palmer (half lemonade, half iced tea), and while we waited for the drinks, he pointed at a tray of cookies in the bakery case behind me. "This place has the *best* snickerdoodles." He reached around me to open the door, and we did an awkward sort of dance, where I shuffled to one side to make room, only he moved in the same direction. Then we shuffled back the other direction. Being so close to him felt embarrassing and exciting at the same time. Finally he gently grabbed my arm and said, "Stay right there." Sort of leaning against me, he reached into the self-serve bakery case and carefully plucked out the largest snickerdoodle cookie with the tongs.

I'd never known a cookie could be so sexy.

After he paid for it, he broke it in half and handed a half to me. "You have to have some. It's the law."

"Snickerdoodle law? I haven't heard of that," I said. I took a small bite. The cookie almost melted in my mouth. "Delicious. Wow. I love cinnamon." I laughed. "That's funny. See, I have a cat named Cinnamon," I said. "What about you? Any pets?"

"We have a couple of goldens," he said. "Golden retrievers, I mean. Best dogs in the world. In fact, I wish I could bring them up here for the summer."

"A dog summer vacation?" I asked. "That would be cool. They'd love it here, right? All this space to run around. They could swim in the lake . . . send postcards home to all their dog-park friends . . ."

He laughed. "You have a dog too?" he asked.

I nodded. "Yep. And it's my job to take him to the off-leash park. And on walks to the park. And pretty much everything. I actually really *miss* him, though."

He looked at me. He smiled. "Yeah? Is there anyone else you miss?"

"Oh, no, well. My family, I guess," I said. What was he asking? Was he trying to find out if I had a boyfriend or something like that? "And, of course, Cinnamon."

"Right." He smiled.

I think I was talking too much, which was so weird, because I'd never had that problem before with a boy. Never ever.

As we turned to walk back to the table with our drinks, we brushed against each other and I felt the same nervous energy I'd felt the first time we made contact, by the cookie case.

Don't get carried away. It's probably just static electricity. Don't be ridiculous. You don't even know anything about him.

Except that you kind of really, really like him . . .

CHAPTER 9

Lucy

"When did you get so bad at tennis?" I asked Claire as we walked into the cabin. After dinner with my grandparents, we'd met up for tennis at the high school courts.

"What? I was fine," Claire said. "You were the one who hit every ball into the court next to ours."

"Me? What about you?" I cried. "You served halfway to Canada! If I had to say 'Little help?' to that couple on the court next to us one more time, I was going to die of shame." I set my racket next to the coat closet inside the front door.

"So, nice shack you got here," Claire observed as she wandered around the living room and peered down the hall toward the bedrooms. "You know, when I first heard about this place from your grandmother, I wished I could live here with you, but now? Not so much."

"What are you talking about? This place is great," I said. "Okay, it still needs some work, but I think in another week or two it could be okay. So how's your job going?" I asked Claire. She worked at a soup-and-sandwich spot, one of the places that stayed open year-round.

"It's pretty good. Same as the winter but ten times busier, so I have to get faster. And how's the Apple Store?" she asked.

"It's okay. It's weird, actually," I confessed.

"Well, after three years of dreading running into Jackson, now you're working with him. So how could it not be weird?" Claire asked.

"Three years." I thought about the Windex he sprayed in my eyes, the melting candles, the awkward silences. But there were a few times we'd laughed, too, so maybe we were getting a little more comfortable around each other. Not that it was saying much.

"It's not as bad as you'd think," I said. "As long as I don't remember how stupid I felt about making a move on him when I was thirteen." I'd never told Claire the long version of the story—the one where I ended up feeling really angry at Jackson. I'd always tried to brush it off as no big deal, just an awkward kiss. The only ones who knew the whole story were

Ava and Mikayla.

"He probably doesn't think about it. Not anymore. He probably forgot," Claire said. "Look at it this way. He's kissed a hundred girls since then."

"Seriously? A hundred?" I couldn't believe that. "What kind of guy is he?"

"So maybe not a hundred, okay? But I saw him last summer with at least a couple different girls—he was working at the Beach Club and they'd come into the deli all the time after work for sandwiches and drinks and stuff. Not that they ever talked to me that much, but the guy is *really* handsome, Luce. The fact you even kissed him once is a major coup. I mean, I'm impressed."

"Don't be. I don't think it's something to brag about if the guy says, 'Yeah, um, *don't*.'"

Claire laughed. "Yeah, but it *counts*."

"Are we counting now?" I asked.

"We're only counting the good ones," Claire said. "Not my prom date a few weeks ago. He reminded me of our Saint Bernard."

"Big and furry?" I asked.

"Slobbery." She shook her head, and I laughed. "I couldn't get inside the house fast enough. I needed a towel."

I tossed the dish towel at her and we both cracked up. "At

least you had a date. I mean, a guy. I went with Mikayla and a bunch of other girls."

"Sounds like a way better plan," Claire said. "I bet you had a blast."

I thought about the manicures, the dress shopping, the limo ride, and how Mikayla and I stole Ava away not only from her slightly pushy senior date but also from her ex, Dean, who kept trying to get her alone "just to talk." After dancing nonstop at prom we'd all gotten a ride home from my dad, who took us out for a midnight breakfast before letting us crash at his house in a pile of sleeping bags on the living room floor. Ava called the night "epic" so many times that we couldn't stop naming all the things that had been epic about it, like: the awkward way her date danced, the fact three girls were wearing the same exact dress, the pancakes and bacon. All of it was epic, which didn't leave much room for improvement for our senior prom.

"Yeah, we did have a great time—still, it would have been nice to go with a guy, too. I mean, how can it be that my parents, who should be too old for stuff like this, can totally find people to fall in love with and get married to, when I can't even have one decent prom date? Is that fair?" I asked Claire.

"It's messed up is what it is," she said. "I can't believe your parents are both getting married."

"Neither can I," I said. "If only my mom didn't talk about her wedding all the time, maybe I could not think about it for a day or two." Earlier that afternoon she'd called to make sure she had my shoe size right because she was going to get a pair of satin pumps dyed for my maid of honor duties—which was crazy, because I didn't even have a *dress* yet that she could match them to. At least, not that I knew of.

My mom is a perfectionist. When she has a plan in mind—like coordinating an outfit, or a wedding—she obsesses over it, and everything has to be about that plan. Like now, with her wedding to Gary, who she met because they're both real estate agents at the same office. They want to sell houses together as a team once they get married: Kerri and Gary. Spouses who sell houses. Sometimes I felt like Mom only wanted to marry Gary because it would look good on their business cards.

Even if Gary is a nice guy, there's something about the born salesman thing that comes to my mind whenever he's talking to me. "It'll be great, this'll be great. Tell you what we're gonna do, Lucy. We're gonna give you fifteen percent off breakfast. And we're gonna throw in clean towels!"

I wasn't going to say anything to Claire or anyone else about it, but I didn't feel ready for Mom and Gary to get married. They'd only been together seven months or so. They were rushing. Part of me wondered if Mom was in such a hurry because Dad was getting remarried at the same time, and she wanted to show him up. The fact they were still so competitive about things after being apart for two years said a lot to me: one, no wonder they couldn't stay married; two, they each cared what the other was up to—more than a little.

I think Mom wanted to have the "better" wedding, while Dad and his fiancée, Margaret, didn't care. They wanted to be married soon, because she had a couple of younger kids, Charlie and Rosie, and her first husband had been killed in a helicopter crash while fighting in Afghanistan. Dad was ready to be an official stepdad to them, and I was happy to share him. I was really looking forward to having those cute little guys as stepsiblings—I hoped they'd eventually consider me their sister, because I'd always kind of wanted to be a big sister. It was messy, and too bad it had to happen this way, but maybe something really good would come out of having two families.

I heard the front door open and turned around to see Mikayla walk into the house. "Hey!" I greeted her. "How was the coffee shop?"

"It was . . . good." Mikayla wandered closer, kind of staring off into the distance, a dreamy expression on her face.

"Mikayla?" I prompted. "You still with us?"

"Oh—yeah. Sorry." She collapsed into one of our folding chairs and sighed. "I have to tell you. I met someone there. Someone, like, that I already have a serious crush on."

"You met him?" I asked. "Like, you actually talked to him?"

She nodded. "I *did*. I mean, it started out kind of awkward—like things usually do with me. But then it turned a corner somehow and we started having a real conversation. And it was easy."

"Wow. So what's his name?" I asked.

"I don't know . . . ," Mikayla said slowly, sort of in a daze.

"You didn't get his *name*?" Claire asked.

"No," she said, slowly shaking her head.

"Well. That sounds promising," I teased.

Mikayla laughed. "I screwed that up, didn't I? But there was a big group, and everyone kind of knew each other, and—gosh. How did I not get his name? You know what? I don't think he got my name either."

"So how are you going to find him?" Claire asked. "Wait for him to leave a shoe behind and then you can track him down and see if it fits? Although, seriously, guys' shoes? Not something you want to carry around."

"Just my luck, right? I meet someone and it turns into a Cinderella situation. Although I doubt he'd appreciate being compared to Cinderella," Mikayla said. "It's weird. I almost ran into him on my bike earlier this week. And he tried to give me his phone number then, but I didn't want it, because he was making too big a deal about whether I was hurt or not. Now, I need it," she said. "Of course then I'd have to get up the nerve to call him, but . . ."

"Not really," said Claire. "Just text."

"Same difference," Mikayla said.

"So you've seen him twice, then?" I asked.

She nodded. "I totally know this might just be in my head. It probably is. But it feels like we have this connection, like . . . I don't know. There's something there. I can't describe it."

"Maybe it's one of those pheromone deals I saw on *Dr. Oz*," Claire said.

"You watch *Dr. Oz*?"

"Only when I'm home with the flu. You can't believe how much this one secret mysterious substance controls your whole entire life."

"Sorry," Mikayla said. "I don't listen to anyone who goes on TV in his pajamas."

"They're not pj's! They're scrubs. He's a surgeon, you know. Half the reason I want to go to med school and help people is because of him. Well, and his TV deal," Claire said.

"Since when are you going premed?" I asked. "Last I knew you wanted to major in French."

"Last year, yeah. Before I knew better," said Claire.

Mikayla sighed. "I wonder where he's staying this summer."

"He who? Dr. Oz? I think he's a bit old for you—"

"No! The guy I met tonight," Mikayla said, laughing at Claire.

"Well, when you don't know someone's name, it's hard to actually talk to them about anything like where they live, isn't it?" Claire teased her.

"I talked to him a lot," Mikayla said.

"You?" I said.

"Well, yeah. He was even flirting with me. At least, I think so." Mikayla's eyes were shining with excitement. I had a feeling she wasn't going to get much sleep that night. "I've got to text Ava right now. Oh, and by the way, Sarah picked me up, she came in for a tour, and she wants to use our house as, like, Party Warehouse."

I didn't get it. "Party Warehouse? Like, we have to sell balloons and plastic forks and graduation tablecloths and Halloween costumes?"

We all started laughing. "No! I meant . . . I meant . . ." Mikayla was laughing so hard she couldn't spit it out. Finally she said, "Party *Central*. Since we have the place to ourselves. I don't know where the warehouse part came from."

"You have boy brain," Claire said. "It's okay. And I guess we know what this means."

"What? Dr. Oz was right?"

"No. We should have gone to Earl Grey's instead of the tennis courts!"

"I missed tennis?" Mikayla asked, looking up.

"No, not really," I said, laughing, thinking that you couldn't really call our game *tennis*. More like five-is.

Maybe my summer hadn't gotten off to the start I wanted it to, but I was definitely excited for Mikayla. And maybe the guy she'd met had a friend.

Hey, it could happen. It happened to other girls all the time. Maybe it was our turn.

CHAPTER 10

Mikayla

Wednesday at noon, I rode my bike out to the Club beach. It was my first day off since Sunday, but I was headed there because a bunch of people had talked about playing volleyball. It was probably a ridiculous idea, but if there was any chance the mystery guy might be there . . . I hadn't managed to run across him, despite the fact I'd ridden my bike all over town—multiple times—in the past three days.

When you wanted to be hit by a car driven by a cute guy, it would never happen. I'd learned that. Maybe that was a good thing, but I was starting to feel pretty hopeless. I'd even pathetically gone to Earl Grey's with Lucy the night before, hoping I'd run into him. It was like he'd vanished into thin air. I hadn't seen him anywhere.

I'd been about to lose hope. I figured he'd bailed and gone back home, due to the fact I'd semi-stolen his job.

I knew I could just ask Henry and Sarah who he was and where he worked, but I didn't want to mess things up. I'd only been in town a week and a half—and at the Club for a week. I didn't want to be *that* girl. The one who showed up and assumed everything that existed was there for her to take.

I'd spent the morning talking to my family, who I was missing more than I thought I would. "Be careful," my mom said at the end of the call. "Don't do anything you're going to regret."

I don't know what she thought was going on up here. "I can assure you, Mom," I said. "It's really no different from home."

I waved at Liam as I rode past him at the gate and on through the parking lot, to the end of the beach with the volleyball net. I leaned my bike against a tree and took off my helmet, shaking out my hair.

When I looked up, I realized it wasn't *just* club people playing. He was at the net. Whoever he was. Cute Near-Car-Crash Coffee-Shop Guy.

That was a really long nickname. I definitely needed to learn his real one.

He was looking at me. Kind of staring, actually. I wasn't sure whether to wave or say hi. Both seemed awkward, so I didn't do either, which was probably just as weird. Instead I immediately looked down and walked over to stand by the net and observe.

We didn't say anything initially. But when Sarah had to go back inside to work, I took her spot—which was right beside him, in front at the net.

"Hey. Where've you been hiding?"

"Hiding? Me? I'm here every day," I said, feeling nervous just to be around him again.

"I haven't seen you around town," he said.

I smiled. If he only knew *how* around town I'd been, looking for *him*.

"What's so funny?" he asked, coming closer to give me a little hip check.

"Nothing. Just—what are you doing here?" I asked as we started to play. "Did you come to get your old job back?"

"Ha. No such luck. It's just my day off," he said.

I hit the ball out of bounds. We lost the point and he turned to me. "Didn't you say something once about playing a lot of sports?" he teased me.

"Hey, I just got here!" I said, laughing. "I'm warming up." A minute later, I jumped up and nailed a spike at the net, making Henry lunge for it and fall into the sand. "That better?" I asked.

"Not cool, Mikayla!" Henry yelled to me. "Not cool!"

"Wow. You have a serious spike," Near-Car-Crash Guy commented as we started the next point. "I'll set you up next time."

"Sounds like a plan," I said.

"You play on a team?" he asked.

I nodded. "I'm kind of the team captain."

"Stand back, people!" he told everyone, holding up his hands. "We have a ringer here, we have a ringer. I'm so glad you're on my team."

"Same here," I said. "I mean, that you're . . . on mine." Fortunately it was my time to serve, so I got to do something besides say embarrassing things. We really got into the game after that, playing for a good half hour before stopping for a break after winning the first match 15 to 9.

I snagged my water bottle from my bike and walked back toward the group, taking a few swigs. "I can't believe how hot it got," I said.

"You're good. Really good," said Henry. "You weren't making that up!"

"Why would I make something up?" I asked.

"Jackson, you totally lucked out," Henry said. "Having

her on your team."

"No doubt," the guy who I'd only known as Near-Car-Crash Guy until now said, reaching over to tug the end of my ponytail. His name is Jackson? It was like my ears suddenly went on full alert. Did Henry really just say *Jackson*?

I gulped, choking on the water I was about to swallow. "You okay?" he asked, patting me on the back and startling me.

Jackson was a common name. Besides, he'd be at work right now with Lucy, wouldn't he? This couldn't be *her* Jackson.

I tried to put the pieces together in my mind. What did her Jackson look like, anyway? Did I even know? She'd never shown me a picture and I hadn't—

A volleyball from the next court over sailed out of bounds. "Heads up, Mik—"

The ball hit me smack in the face. On the nose, to be more precise. "Ow!" I cried.

"Yikes. You okay?" Jackson asked.

"Oh, I'm fine!" I said, gently pressing my nose. When my hand came away there wasn't any blood, but it did feel like it was beginning to swell a little. Plus, I needed time to recover from learning Jackson's name. "I'm going to go get some ice—be right back!" I called, rushing toward the Club's kitchen building. But as much as my nose stung, I was more worried about whether the guy I'd been falling for was the same one Lucy worked with—the one she'd been cursing ever since eighth grade.

While I was inside, I was going to make an important call.

I didn't want to know, but I had to find out if this Jackson was the same as Lucy's Jackson. The odds were against it. Sure, he was going to be a senior in high school, like us. But so were half the people I'd met so far. Anyway, there were at least three guys I knew back home named Jackson. I'd just call Lucy and put my mind at ease.

I found a quiet nook in the hallway outside the restroom and dialed Lucy's cell number. She didn't answer, so I looked up the Apple Store and called that number. It was obnoxious, but I had to do it, even if she was really busy.

Please let a guy answer, I thought. *Please*. A guy with a nice, deep voice, a guy with a high, awkward voice—just *not* an old voice belonging to her grandfather, because that wouldn't solve anything.

"The Apple Store, this is Lucy, how may I help you?"

"Hey," I said nervously, wishing Jackson had picked up instead. "How's it going?"

"You won't believe this, but an entire family reunion from Montana was just here."

"Why would I not believe that?" I asked.

"It was like thirty or forty people!" she laughed. "And who has a family reunion in Bridgeport? Especially when they don't live anywhere near here?"

"Are you sure it wasn't a wedding?" I asked.

"Unless the bride and groom were sixty-five? Then no."

"Could be," I said. "I mean, it could take *me* that long," I joked.

"Your voice sounds funny," Lucy commented. "Are you coming down with a cold or something?"

"No, I got hit by a volleyball. In the nose," I admitted.

"You? Prep star of the week?" Lucy asked.

"Totally embarrassing, I know."

"But wait, aren't you off work today?"

"Yeah, but I came down here to the beach and ran into some friends," I said. "So how are things with . . . you know. Mr. Awkward?" I asked.

"Who, Jackson? He's not here today. It's just me and my nana."

I felt my legs go kind of wobbly. "Oh, really? He's not there?" I asked, hoping maybe I'd heard wrong.

"Nope," she said in a softer voice, "and I love my grandmother but she is working me to death."

"Huh," was about all I could say. "Okay, well, if you get a break, text me—maybe we can meet up? See you later!" I sort of slumped against the wall. What was I going to do about the fact that I'd had three major interactions with this really cute guy named Jackson . . . and Lucy's Jackson was not at work, which meant . . . we were talking about the same Jackson. We had to be.

"Hey, are you okay?"

I turned around, and Jackson was standing behind me. "Did you find an ice pack? Maybe it's broken. Let me see." He put his hand on my face, his palm warm and gentle as he lightly pressed my cheeks and nose.

I'd never stood so close to a boy before. Ever. Unless I was eight and trying to tackle him in flag football. I felt shivers go down my back when he touched me. Who needed an ice pack? My body had broken out in goose bumps.

"I don't think it is," he said. "And actually, it doesn't even feel that swollen. You'll avoid the classic black-and-blue bruise on your face."

"So . . . there's that," I said, trying to breathe normally. He backed up a little and I said, "Okay, so this is kind of weird, because I've talked to you a couple of times already. But I didn't even know what your name was until a minute ago."

"Jackson," he said. "You're Mikayla, right?"

I nodded, in a daze, and he started telling a story about

how he'd broken his nose playing peewee football, but I could hardly listen as we walked back outside, thoughts swirling in my head.

So this was Lucy's Jackson, the guy who'd been a jerk to her and convinced her she should never attempt to kiss anyone again.

He'd been acting really nice to me. He'd been flirting with me, and I'd been attempting to flirt back, and for some reason when I was around him I felt different, like we really connected, and I *could* talk to him.

But maybe he wasn't what he seemed. If the way he'd treated Lucy was any indication, I should probably keep my distance—starting now.

On the other hand, all I'd seen of Jackson so far made me think he was a nice, considerate person. He could have changed in the past three years. And he and Lucy had been friends for years before their falling-out. Maybe he'd just had a temporary lack of good judgment.

"Anyway," he said, wrapping up his story, "I thought for sure my nose was going to be crooked but somehow it turned out all right. I'm sure yours will too. So what were you daydreaming about?"

"Daydreaming? Me?" I joked. "I never do that."

"That's why you got bopped in the nose, isn't it? Or were

you calculating how to win the next game?" Jackson asked, smiling at me.

"Pretty much," I said. There was no way I'd tell him why I really blanked out. "That and I was super hot at the same time. Probably wasn't thinking straight."

"Sunstroke, or what?" he asked, sounding confused.

Yeah, that's it. The heat. Actually, more like you. Even as I thought that, I knew I had to stay away from him. Not just because of the way he'd acted toward Lucy a while back, but because it would be too upsetting to Lucy now. The last thing I wanted to do was hurt her.

"So before we get back in the game and you get all distracted and break some other bone," Jackson teased, "do you want to do something sometime? Like maybe one night this weekend?"

I nodded. "Um, maybe." I probably should have just said no, straight off the bat, but I didn't have a reason to give if he asked. "Why not?" Not a reason I felt comfortable telling him, anyway.

Except for this flock of nervous butterflies in my tummy, it sounded really good. But I couldn't get together with Jackson until I talked it over with Lucy—and if I told Lucy I was interested in him, she'd tell me to stay away from him.

I didn't even know if I *could* walk away.

CHAPTER 11

Lucy

"Where's Mikayla?" Claire asked when we sat down at a table on the Walleye Mafia deck on Thursday night.

The deck is right beside the lake and has incredible views of the shore; on weekends it's impossible to get a table without waiting an hour or more. But since it was a Thursday night, Claire and I had managed to score a table with no problem.

"She had to help with a cookout at work," I said. "It's Parents' Night Out. I'm surprised this place isn't packed with parents, actually."

We had both just decided what we wanted from the menu when Jackson walked up wearing khakis, a crisp white button-down shirt, and one of those black aprons that tie around your waist so you can keep pens and order pads inside.

"Welcome. Tonight's special is a smoked trout sandwich with marinara sauce," he said.

I tried not to laugh, but he was doing that official waiter talk and it just didn't suit him.

"You have two jobs?" I asked, incredulous.

"Yeah, I just got a new car. I have to make the payments," he said.

"Tell me about it. I'll be paying my parents back for the next three years," said Claire.

"Um, nice khakis. You're sort of dressed up for this gig," I said to Jackson.

"Hey, at least I'm not wearing a red apple shirt. Right *now*, anyway. So you guys eating here?"

I rolled my eyes. "No, we just dropped by to hang out with you and take up table space. Of course we're eating here."

"Okay, so the special is trout? You out of walleye or what?" asked Claire.

"Nah, trout is just the special because it was freshly caught. Can I take your order, or should I give you a few more minutes to look at the menu?" he asked.

"Seriously?" I said. "Who are you?"

"I have to say this stuff, okay?" He poked my shoulder with the pen he was carrying. "I might get rated by mystery shoppers."

"Mystery diners?" Claire suggested.

"Whatever. Reviewers," Jackson said. He sort of blushed.

"But wouldn't you know that we're not—them?" I asked.

"Maybe it's her job, how should I know? I'll come back in a few minutes to take your order," he said. "But take your time, there's no rush." He gave a little half smile and moved on to the next table.

"That was awkward," Claire commented.

"Really?" I took a sip of ice water. "This is a lot better than it was a couple of days ago."

"I don't know, Lucy. You guys act pretty weird around each other, as if you kind of like each other and kind of don't. I'm pretty sure that's a classic sign of sexual attraction."

"Like you would know!" I teased her, laughing. "Yeah . . . no." I shook my head. "That's because we only started talking again a few days ago. So it's still awkward but it's improving slightly."

"No, that's not it. I think there's still a spark between you guys," Claire commented. "Isn't there?"

I laughed. "If that's a spark, I'd like to see the fire it would start. That would be a pretty pathetic fire."

I held my finger to my lips as I saw Jackson approaching our table again. There was no way I wanted him to overhear this. Claire ordered a meatball sandwich, while I opted for the walleye panini.

"Here's what happened," I said after he left. I scooted my chair closer to the table so I could talk to her softly.

I told her how we'd been friends for a long time—she knew that part already. We had done everything together, up to a point. When middle school started, there was a big group of us that hung out, going to movies, the mall, wherever. We had pizza parties; we went to school events, dances, football games. We did field trips to language camp; we went camping as part of the seventh-grade Explorers Club; and on weekends at the end of eighth grade, we all hung out at Highland Pool.

Every once in a while, one couple or another would sort of form for a few weeks, then they'd break up or maybe they wouldn't—but nobody was serious about "dating."

Jackson and I were hanging out at the pool one Saturday, a week before graduation. We'd been goofing around a lot in the water, playing chicken against other friends with me perched on his shoulders, and after some crashes and dunks and tickling, I was starting to feel like more than friends with him.

After we dried off in the sun for a while, we both went into the rec building to get something to drink from the vending machine. For some reason that was when I'd decided to make my move. I stepped toward him and kissed him.

"How did you reach?" asked Claire.

"He was shorter then. This was pre—major growth spurt." I blushed, just thinking in detail about that day.

"Love by the vending machine," Claire said. "How romantic."

"Sounds tacky, I know. So, okay, he said, 'Um, don't.' Totally humiliating. He took off, leaving me there with my Diet Coke, feeling like a complete fool."

Claire studied me. "Why is the Diet Coke important in this story?"

I laughed, grateful that she could see the humor in this. Now I could too, in a way. The next part? Not so much. I'd gone back out to the pool and acted like everything was normal for the rest of the day, but I knew things with Jackson wouldn't be the same for a while. We kept our distance and sort of migrated to hanging out with other people in the group.

Then I got to school the next Monday. Before I knew it, I started hearing rumors—about myself. About how I made a pass at him, and how I was desperately in love with him and wouldn't stop following him around. None of it was true, especially the part about me sobbing. I was so mad that I decided never to talk to him again.

Then we graduated from middle school, and I switched schools, and he switched schools, but it didn't even matter. Some people followed me to my new school, so even though Jackson wasn't there, the rumor persisted.

About ten minutes later, after I'd finished telling Claire about it, Jackson delivered our food, setting the plates carefully in front of us. "Is there anything else I can bring you right now?"

"No," Claire said firmly.

"I'll make sure you get some fresh water, and then I'll check with you in a few minutes to see how you're doing," he said.

"We'll be fine," Claire said. "We don't need fresh water. We're not fish."

Jackson stepped back a little, looking surprised by her tone. "Okay," he said. "If that's what you want."

"Claire!" I said after he left. "Did you have to be so rude?"

"After what you just told me? Yeah. It makes me not want to give him a tip. It makes me want to write a really bad review of the service here," she said. "How can you work with him?"

"It was a while ago, and I guess I'm starting to forgive him," I said, "as weird as that sounds."

"Good for you, because I don't know if I would," she replied.

"I don't have much choice. My nana hired him, and if I want a job this summer . . . she's not going to let him go just because it's awkward for me. I already asked."

We both started laughing. "You didn't," Claire said.

I nodded. "I did. Hey, it was worth a shot. So in answer to your question, no. There's no spark." Jackson was good-looking. He was probably still smart, unless he had changed a lot. Then again, he couldn't figure out how to ring up candles that were three for five dollars when someone only wanted two of them. He was kind to my grandparents. But did I like him? No.

"So how about Mikayla? Did she find out who that mystery guy was yet?" Claire asked.

"No, she hasn't mentioned him again, so I guess not. Just her luck. I mean, sometimes I think I'm shy and I have a hard time meeting boys? And then I see her and it's, like, physically painful for her."

"Well, it's still early in the summer. She'll probably see him again. This town isn't that big. Take it from someone who lives here year-round."

My phone buzzed with a text and I glanced down at it, hoping it was Ava. Every time I'd tried to contact her lately, I'd failed; either I caught her at a really busy time and she had to call back, or she responded with a short message that didn't tell me anything about how she was. I was starting to worry about her.

Thinking about a trip to visit you, my mom had written.

Mom, I've only been gone for 10 days, I wrote back.

10 long days! Plus, need your opinion. Centerpieces. Orchids or roses?

Roses, I texted. Then I turned off my alerts and put my phone facedown on the table. It was time to sit back, visit with Claire, and enjoy the famous deck view. Somehow it felt better to have told Claire the story from beginning to end. No matter what my grandmother might think, it really *was* a long time ago. Time to put it behind me for good, and move on. "So. What are we doing this weekend?" I asked.

CHAPTER 12

Mikayla

"What is the par for this course?" I asked.

"Three. And this is your eighth shot." Lucy laughed. "What is the deal? You've never been this bad at mini golf before. Or, actually, anything."

"It's because my arms are so tired. I had to help carry in all the sailing stuff today," I said.

"Then you should be good at this hole," Lucy said.

I glared at her as my golf ball bounced off a wooden toy sailboat that kept circling a fake, blue-painted lake. You had to sneak your shot past while three boats were rotating and get it through the lighthouse in order to get to the putting green. I was stuck. "How about you get me through this one?" I asked Lucy, who'd already finished the hole. "Then can we *please* stop playing and get something to eat?"

"Love to," she said. She lined up the shot, tapped the ball, and sent it caroming off the side, past the boat and through the lighthouse.

"Sometimes I really hate you," I said.

"Right. But you need me," Lucy said, laughing.

I put my putter on my shoulder. "Let's call it a game."

"Thought you'd never ask."

Lucy and I walked over to the wooden shack and turned in our golf balls and clubs, then headed to Midge's right next door. Midge's had the best ice cream in Bridgeport, according to Lucy. I hadn't tasted nearly enough ice cream so far that summer to be sure.

A few couples were lingering outside at picnic tables. Just as Lucy and I walked up to the window to order, a car pulled up and about six guys climbed out. One of them was wearing a St. Paul Saints T-shirt, which made me think of Jackson— he'd been wearing a shirt for the same baseball team when we played beach volleyball.

I'd been having such a good time hanging out with Lucy that I'd almost—almost—forgotten about Jackson and how much I wanted to see him again.

Thankfully I'd gotten control of my emotions where

Jackson was concerned.

I wasn't going to see him. I'd been avoiding him for the past two days, staying away from the coffee shop. Not hanging out at the Club after work. If I avoided visiting Lucy at work too, I could just keep my distance until this whole thing cooled down.

Lucy nudged me and raised her eyebrows as the guys came up behind us in line.

I nudged her back gently with my elbow. "What are you going to get?"

"Small hot fudge sundae with banana walnut ice cream," she said. "You?"

"Mint chocolate chip in a cone," I said. "Maybe a triple."

"You wouldn't dare," Lucy said.

"I'm hungry!" I said. But when I got my cone a minute later, I could see why she'd been so worried. We both burst out laughing as the server handed it to me. The ice-cream cone was so tall, it barely fit through the take-out window.

"You need some help with that?" one of the boys behind us in line asked as I walked past.

"No—uh," I mumbled.

"Because we could split it," he said.

"No—uh," I said again. I rolled my eyes—at myself—as I gingerly carried the giant tower of ice cream.

"Don't mind her," Lucy said. "She's a foreign-exchange student." She hurried after me toward a picnic table. "You're going to drop it!" Lucy said, laughing.

"What did they do, put a whole gallon on here? There's no way I can even, like, hold this!" I laughed.

Lucy pulled her phone out of her shorts pocket and took a picture of the gargantuan cone, then checked her messages. With my non-cone hand, I scrolled through Facebook posts and updates, checking out what my friends and family were up to back home.

While Lucy was busy texting, I quickly turned to the side and looked up Jackson's profile. His privacy settings kept me from seeing too much. Still, I couldn't find anything about him I didn't like—the only mark against him that I could see (*not* on Facebook) was the fact he'd ruined Lucy's life for a while. That wasn't easy to overlook. Still, maybe it wasn't a big deal anymore. They were young then. We weren't now. It wasn't like she had talked about still having a crush on him or anything—she'd moved on.

Right?

"Anything good?" Lucy asked, glancing up. Her eyes widened. "Mikayla!" she cried.

"What?" I instantly turned over my phone, worried she'd seen me checking out Jackson and his friends.

"Look at the table!"

There was a large pool of green ice cream spreading wider and wider, while my hand was covered with mint chip. I'd gotten so wrapped up in scanning Facebook that I'd neglected to eat my cone.

Lucy ran to get more napkins and a dish for me, while the guy sitting one table over with his friends said, "I offered to help, you know."

"Yeah, I don't know what she was thinking," Lucy said as she returned. "Clearly she needs help."

He smiled back and then laughed, shaking his head, while Lucy began to clean me up. I felt like a little kid, like my stepbrothers used to be: they'd wear half of their ice cream instead of eating it. So. Totally. Embarrassing.

"What were you looking at, anyway?" Lucy asked.

"Oh, the usual stuff." I turned my phone over and immediately went back to my own Facebook page, where my mom had posted a new photo of my half sister, Anya, posed with our dog, who she'd dressed up in a hat and scarf. I held it out to show Lucy. "Cute, right?"

"So where are you guys from?" The group of boys just sort of converged on us, some of them sitting at the table next to ours, while others stood around our table.

"M-Minneapolis?" I said.

He looked askance at Lucy. "I thought you said she was a foreign-exchange student."

"Her English is really terrible," Lucy said. "Don't let her fool you."

"Um, she didn't," he said. "You guys just visiting then?"

"We're here for the whole summer. Working in Bridgeport," Lucy said. I just kept attempting to eat my ice-cream cone while staying out of the conversation. She didn't need my help. She needed me *not* to help. "How about you?"

"Up for the summer. We're staying in Kingfield."

"That's cool." Lucy nodded. "You guys going to play mini golf?"

"We might. Are you?"

"We actually just did. So, anyway, we have to go now." She pulled at my sleeve as she walked past me. "So. Embarrassing," she said once we got into the car and closed the doors behind us.

We started laughing, out-of-control laughing, the kind that hurts your stomach. She quickly finished her sundae so that she could drive, and we pulled out of the lot.

"Look at your face! It's still part green," she said, laughing.

"Since when am I a foreign-exchange student?" I said. "Where am I supposed to be from?"

"I don't know. Mars?" she suggested, and we burst out laughing again.

That was the thing about Lucy: not only was she a great and true friend, she was always able to make me laugh. It was killing me to not blurt out that I'd met Jackson. I wanted to tell her. But how could I risk hurting her when I wasn't even sure if Jackson actually wanted to see me—and if he did, whether I was special to him or just one girl out of many he liked.

I knew I couldn't keep this secret from her for much longer, but for right now, I was keeping my mouth closed. As far as I knew, soon Lucy and I would both be trying to meet boys all over again.

CHAPTER 13

Lucy

A crack of thunder boomed outside and a bright flash of lightning lit up the store's plate-glass window for a second. "Somehow I don't think we're going to sell anything today," I said.

"I hope it stops. I have to work tonight. Not much of a deck view right now," Jackson said.

"On the other hand, the walleye could just, like, swim onto the deck. Talk about fresh."

Jackson stopped organizing the greeting cards and postcards in the racks by the front window and peered out the doors at the pouring rain. "It's not completely hopeless," he said in a cheerful voice, as if the fact we were in the middle of a tropical storm was just fine with him.

"Just mostly hopeless, then?" I said.

He laughed. "It is kind of monsoonlike, actually. Do you think we're still supposed to clean the front windows and sweep the sidewalk?"

"Only if you can do it without drowning," I said. "Maybe use a sponge?"

"Well, at least we're not working on a sales commission. We get paid whether anyone buys apple stuff or not."

"Apple stuff?" I asked. "Maybe my grandparents would like to change the name of the store to that."

"Seriously. They should think about changing it to something else. I took, like, ten calls yesterday from people wanting help with their iPads," said Jackson.

"And? Did you help them?" I asked.

"I told them they had the wrong number," he said. "Except for a couple really easy fixes. Some people are so clueless. I didn't want them to embarrass themselves by actually calling Apple."

"You still good at that?" I asked. Then I realized: one thing we never actually did was acknowledge that we knew each other before this summer. We never, ever talked about who we were at home, or who we used to be.

That makes it sound like we had secret identities. Not the case. We just didn't admit to there being any history between us. Or at least *I* didn't. One day I was going to have to talk to Jackson about how much he'd hurt me.

"Yeah, I know some things," Jackson said. "Not like I'm going to major in computer science or anything."

There was an awkward pause. A long one. *You can do this*, I said to myself. *You can have a conversation with Jackson about something besides apples. And the weather.* Just because I hadn't seen him in three years didn't mean I didn't still basically *know* him. "So what *do* you want to major in?" I asked.

"I'm thinking economics," he said. "Maybe accounting." He shrugged. "Maybe the biology of apples."

"Is that, like, a thing?" I asked. "Wait, it's called botany."

"How would I know? You should know," he said. "You're good at science. You used to kill me on tests, anyway."

There it was again. The past. Yes, it existed. Could we just move on already?

"So are you still into science?" he asked.

I nodded. "I like it. I like history and politics, too. I'm not sure which I'll end up doing. We have a while to decide, though."

"Not that long," he said. "I mean, we'll have to start applying in the fall."

"We will," I agreed.

He nodded. I nodded. It was a nod-a-thon.

We went back to our boring tasks without another word to each other. A few weeks ago, I wouldn't have believed that I could be in the same room with Jackson. Now, here we were having a conversation. It might not be a meaningful one, but we were having it.

The apple-shaped bell over the door started ringing, and I glanced out to see a boy holding an umbrella, which he quickly closed and left by the door. His yellow raincoat nearly had rivers coursing down it.

"You sell apples, right?" he asked, shaking water off his coat over by the door.

Jackson and I shared a funny look. "Um, yeah," Jackson said, launching into his spiel about the various kinds we had in stock, but he was cut short.

"I really hope you can help me." The boy lifted off his hood, revealing short, spiky red-brown hair.

"What do you need?" I asked. I walked away from the register toward him.

He looked over at me as if he hadn't realized I was there too. "Oh, hi." As I got closer I could hear him panting a little bit, as if he'd run the whole way. His cheeks were pink and a single drop of rain was running down the right side of his face.

"Okay, here's the deal. I work for Blue Cove Catering. We

have this major dinner tonight. Wedding reception. Whatever. Anyway, we're supposed to be serving apples and cheese. The apples we were supposed to get from the distributor this morning didn't show up. The apples at the grocery store are too bruised. And the co-op only has Pink Ladies from Washington State and this is supposed to be local."

"We can help," I said. "What do you need?"

"Chef Michael is having a Northern Spy crisis. He says if he can't get ten dozen Northern Spies by noon, it's going to be trouble."

"Sounds like an international incident," Jackson commented. "Or a James Bond movie."

"It's definitely an . . . incident," the boy said. "The wedding's supposed to be outdoors in the first place, so everyone's freaking out about whether the tent they arranged is going to be big enough. Which is totally a valid concern. But then the apples . . . chef's threatening to cancel over the lack of decent Northern Spies."

"Wow. Canceling over apples? *That's* extreme."

"Yeah, he's a little dramatic. And he yells a lot at whoever happens to be nearby, which usually happens to be me, because the only other employee is his mother, from what I can tell," he said, raking his hand through his hair. "So is there any way you have ten dozen perfect Northern Spy apples? And if you don't, can you tell me who might?"

"We should have close to that," I said. "Let's go take a look in the back. Jackson, can you bag up what we have out here?"

I walked into the cold storage room, and the boy followed me. "Wow. It's freezing back here!" he commented, rubbing his arms.

"Yeah, this is where we keep the bad apples," I joked.

"It's apple jail?" he said, and we both laughed.

"No, seriously. This is just to keep them fresh." I found the large bin of Northern Spies and was pretty sure we'd have enough. I measured out dozens into a couple of cardboard boxes and a bushel crate with his help. Then Jackson and I combined the amounts we had and stacked them by the front door.

"I just realized something," the boy said as he eyed the boxes. "He gave me no way to pay for all these."

"It's no trouble. I can make out an invoice and you can take it with. He can send a check," I said as I headed to the counter for the paperwork. "If he doesn't, my grandparents will bill him. And if he doesn't pay that . . . you know, apple justice."

"Sounds like the Mafia," he commented.

"Or the Walleye Mafia," Jackson added.

"Yes, but it's much worse," I said. "We actually cut you with an apple corer." He and Jackson laughed. "So you're from . . . where, again? And what's your name?"

"Blue Cove Catering." He quickly gave the address and phone number. "And my name's Gus. And you're potentially saving my life, so thanks." He smiled at me and I noticed he had startlingly green eyes, with little flecks in them.

That flustered me for a second. "No problem." I focused back on the invoice, jotting down the details. I handed him the top copy, then followed him to the door. "Let me help you carry those out."

"I'll get it," said Jackson.

"No, I've got it," I insisted.

Gus lifted the top two boxes and I got the bottom two. Outside, a blue van with the letters *B ue Cove Cat ring* painted on the side was parked at the end of the block. The rain was still coming down pretty hard, but the worst of the thunderstorm seemed to have passed. Gus opened the sliding door and we loaded the boxes, one at a time. I stood back and brushed my hands against my shorts as he closed the door.

"What's a 'cat ring'?" I asked, pointing at the painted logo.

"It's like the Cat Mafia," he said. "But more cruel."

"Right. So, see you around?" I asked, anxious to get back inside.

"Yeah. Sure. Thanks again!" he called.

"No problem!" I jogged back to the store, getting more drenched with every step. I'd need to grab a new dry staff T-shirt—my grandmother would understand.

"Apple emergency," I said to Jackson, drying my hair with a paper towel once I was back inside the store. "Whoever heard of a Northern Spy crisis?"

"Russia?" Jackson asked. "It seemed like this was his first day on the job. Or his last."

"Exactly. I'm so glad I don't have that kind of job. I would not want that much stress." I couldn't believe I had just said that. Two weeks ago this was the most stressful job I could have imagined, but only because of my coworker. To be honest, it still was a little stressful working with Jackson, but at least Gus had helped me put it in perspective. "He sent that poor guy out in the pouring rain to get apples—like it couldn't have waited half an hour or even ten minutes?"

"Chef Michael is in for a surprise, because I put a couple different varieties in the bags I filled. You think that's okay?" Jackson asked.

"What? You did not. Chef Michael is going to come over and kick your butt," I said. "Just watch him."

"It's going to be an apple smackdown?" Jackson asked.

We started laughing. I couldn't help thinking of the time

we'd gone to see a Smackdown event live at the convention center. Monster trucks battling monster Jeeps. We used to think that was cool—when was that? Fourth grade?

After I hurried into the bathroom to quickly change shirts, I came back out and finished doing the paperwork for the invoice, making sure I put the pink and yellow copies in the right box so my grandparents would see them.

I looked at the invoice. *Gus Savoy*, it said in terrible handwriting. Either that or Gus Savory, which would be really weird.

I had a feeling that Gus was going to be a good addition to the summer. Maybe he lived in town all year, and if he did, maybe Claire knew him. I'd have to ask her.

CHAPTER 14

Mikayla

"This is legal, right?" I asked Lucy.

"Of course it is. Don't you trust us?" Claire replied, standing beside her.

"Sure. Sure," I said quickly. "I guess. I'm just not used to such big outdoor fires. They tend to frown on those back home. In fact, there's a guy on our block who got in big trouble for trying something like this."

"Well, sure, when they're in someone's back*yard*," Lucy said. "This is different. If the fire gets too big, we're right beside the lake."

"Plus, the cold, wet sand keeps it from spreading," said Claire.

I looked around Bridgeport's "small" beach (as opposed to

the big, official swimming beach, which was located near the ferry and the center of town), at the fire burning on the sand, surrounded by people perched on rocks. Music blared from somewhere, and there were coolers filled with pop, water— probably other stuff too, but I wasn't up for that. About half of my coworkers were hanging out, along with a lot of other people I didn't know at all.

Since a lot of Jackson's friends were here, I was worried he would be too. Technically, I was more excited than worried, though. I really wanted to see him. More than anything. Not that I could say that to Lucy, or anyone else here.

"The only part that's not legal is maybe what some people are drinking," Lucy said. "But since we're having plain old lemonade, I think we're good."

We started playing a beanbag game, but since it was almost ten o'clock and the moon was new, it was nearly impossible. "Sorry!" I cried as I tossed one right at Claire.

"I can't see what I'm doing. Can any of you guys?" Lucy asked.

"That's what makes it fun!" Claire said.

"No, that's what makes me suck at it," Lucy said. "Come on, let's go sit by the fire. Did anyone bring marshmallows?" she asked as we walked up to the circle to take a seat.

"It's all yours." Henry handed her a roasting stick and a

bag of marshmallows. "I've had about ten in a row and can now go throw up."

"Who has a good ghost story?" Claire asked, while Lucy loaded up the stick with three marshmallows, one for each of us. She handed me the bag to hold.

"Come on. You still believe in ghost stories?" someone replied.

"You don't have to believe to tell one and freak everyone else out," Claire said. "That's the point."

Suddenly I noticed a new face in the group across the fire from us. It was Jackson. He was *here*. I was so startled that I almost dropped the bag of marshmallows into the fire.

"I thought you were working late!" Sarah said.

"I was, but it got dead all of a sudden, so they cut me," Jackson said.

"Love how that restaurant language makes it sound like a death match," Henry commented.

"Hey, it *is* the Mafia," Claire joked.

Jackson glanced over at her and laughed, and that's when he noticed me. Our eyes met across the bonfire. "Hey, Mikayla," he said. "Oh, hey, Lucy."

A log crashed down in the bonfire at that very second, showering us with sparks.

"Oh. Hey." I gave a little wave, acknowledging him very

casually, while inside I was dying of nervousness. He'd said my name, so now Lucy knew that . . .

"Hey!" Lucy called across the bonfire to him. Then she turned to me. "You guys know each other already?"

"We met at the Club," I said quickly. "Just, you know. Playing volleyball."

"Why didn't you tell me?" she asked in a whisper.

"It didn't come up—listen, Lucy, I have to talk to you," I blurted. "Excuse us." I plucked the marshmallow stick from her hand and gave it to Claire, then I half nudged and half dragged Lucy away from the fire, over to the water's edge.

"Uh-oh. Sounds serious," Lucy said. "What's up?"

"I did meet Jackson before. I just didn't tell you because . . ." I heard Jackson laughing, over by the bonfire. This was so hard. I loved his laugh. If I told Lucy I was interested in him, she'd not only hate me, she'd probably give me an earful of why I should avoid him like the plague. Suddenly I lost my nerve on being a hundred percent honest with her.

"You didn't tell me because you thought I'd freak out," Lucy said. "Well, don't worry, I'm not going to."

Relief flooded through me. But it was too early for that, because I hadn't actually said anything important yet. "You're not?"

"Nope," she said. "In fact, it's probably a relief that you know him now."

"Um, why?"

"Because I've only talked about him a dozen times so far this summer," she said out of the corner of her mouth. "Now you can put a face to the name."

"Right." I nodded. That was one advantage. Especially when it was such a nice face.

"I wish you hadn't felt like you needed to hide the fact you knew him. You don't have to confess or anything. We *are* best friends, you know. I won't crumple on you."

"I know, but . . ." I thought about telling her more, like how we'd had a couple of intense up-close moments with each other, and how he'd kind of asked me out only we'd never set an actual date, but I was hoping—

"I'm dying for that marshmallow," Lucy said. "Can we head back? Is there something else, or was that it?"

"That was . . . it?" I didn't sound—or feel—convinced. "I guess. But are you sure? Because only a couple weeks ago you didn't even want to run into him or work with him. That's the only reason I didn't tell you I'd met him."

"I totally appreciate you being concerned, but it's not such a big deal to me anymore. I know I've been acting a little over the top, but it's going better now. I'm not going to let it

define my summer or anything. So come on, let's get back."
She looped her arm through mine and we hurried back to the
bonfire.

Maybe it wasn't that big of a deal to her. I really hoped
that was true.

An hour later, after a couple of marshmallows and a couple of
s'mores, my hands were about as sticky as the kids at the BBC
after lunch. Before I started playing glow-in-the-dark Frisbee,
I needed to clean them off or my hands would stick to the
disc. "Be right back!" I told Lucy and Claire.

I went to the water's edge, waded in, and started running
my hands through the cool water. As I was walking back to
the Frisbee game, Jackson jogged to catch up with me. "Hey.
I haven't had a chance to talk to you yet. Have you been
avoiding me?"

"No. Not at all. I've just been really busy lately," I said.

"Me too. Do you want to go for a walk?" Jackson asked.

"Just us?" I asked.

He nodded. "That's the idea."

"That—um—okay," I said, looking over my shoulder and
wondering where Lucy was. Maybe I hadn't been completely
honest with Lucy about my feelings for Jackson, but at least
I'd gotten one thing cleared up. Now I didn't have to feel so

bad about talking to him, anyway.

"You sure?" Jackson asked, walking backward in front of me. "You didn't sound a hundred percent."

"No, I am," I said. "But it's so late—and where would we go?"

"Down the beach a little—there's a cove, kind of behind those trees. We could walk down there, and back," Jackson said.

"Sure," I said.

"So have you been up here other summers?" Jackson asked as we set out.

"Once, for a week or so," I admitted.

"So how did I not meet you then? You must have hid out," he said.

"I'm good at that," I said. "I'm actually part hermit. It's in my astrological sign."

He groaned. "Don't tell me you believe in that stuff."

"Um . . ."

"You do?"

"No!" I said. "Seriously, I don't. But I still think there are tons of things in life that can't be easily explained." *For instance: Why would I meet you now?*

"You mean, like UFOs," he said.

"No, those are totally fake. Are you serious?" I laughed.

"So you don't believe in aliens, but you still believe in the sign of the tiger," he said.

I burst out laughing. "There's no such thing as a tiger sign. There's a lion—"

"I don't know! Why should I know? It's all made up, anyway." He laughed too. We walked a little bit farther until I tripped on a rock and Jackson grabbed my arm to keep me from falling, but instead of letting go, he took my hand in his and squeezed. We stepped on to the cove's sand and kept walking down the beach, hand in hand.

I didn't believe in love at first sight. It was just a story people told, a fairy tale. But if this wasn't love at first (and second and third) sight, what was it? Since the day Jackson had nearly run me off the road, this was how I felt when I was around him. I couldn't pretend the feeling wasn't there.

"Is this where we have to turn around?" I asked, when we reached the end of the short beach.

"I guess so," Jackson said. "It is late."

"It is," I agreed. We strolled back in the direction of the bonfire. Then we both stopped. Neither one of us seemed to want to go back.

"Hey." Jackson turned to face me. He tucked my hair behind my ears, and ran his hand down the side of my check.

I squeezed his hand more tightly and moved closer to him.

We were looking at each other for a second and then we were kissing, our lips finding each other's as if it wasn't the first time, but like we'd been doing this forever. We fit together like two unusual jigsaw puzzle pieces that you don't have to force: they don't look like a match until you turn them the right way, and then you solve that entire side of the puzzle.

I'd never kissed anyone before. I'd spent hours daydreaming of what it would feel like. But it wasn't anything like what I'd imagined. With Jackson, it felt natural and normal and exciting and incredible all rolled into one. And then some.

We stopped for a second, caught our breath, smiled at each other. I leaned into him, putting my arms around his waist, as he kissed my cheek and my neck.

I didn't want the night to end. Ever.

CHAPTER 15

Lucy

"No! You didn't win." Claire pretended to shove Gus a little bit.

"Oh, yeah. We totally won," he insisted. As it turned out, Gus and Claire were both juniors at Bridgeport High. Since it was a small town, they knew each other pretty well, or at least they'd been in the same schools for years.

"You did not," I said.

"Did too!" Gus cried.

"The thing about these midnight games of Frisbee tag? Is that everyone wins," Claire said. "Especially when I have the best player on my team." She put her arm around my shoulders and we headed toward the bonfire—not that there was much of it left.

"Except when there's no moon and it's impossible to see what's happening," I added. "Then it's dangerous."

"Come on, what's a sprained ankle, anyway?" Henry asked. "My dad would say it's character building."

"So would mine!" added Gus.

"It's not sprained, anyway. Just slightly twisted." Sarah pressed her fingers against her ankle. "Actually, it feels fine."

"Where did Mikayla go?" Henry asked. "She ditched us before the game even started. Then again, a lot of people drifted off, because other than those guys playing Wiffle ball over there, we're the only ones left."

"I'm guessing she went home," I said. "She was pretty tired earlier. She gets up super early in the morning to go running."

"Well, that's no fun," said Sarah. "She's supposed to be organizing a party at your house, not running."

I laughed. "Yeah, I kind of heard about this party we're having. What do I need to know?"

"Why haven't I heard about it?" Gus asked.

"Because it doesn't exist yet. Don't worry, you're definitely invited," I told him, then kind of wished I hadn't said it so loudly. It wasn't that I didn't want to invite him, but it sounded like I was asking him out. "I mean, everyone's invited."

"Even me," Gus said. "Aha. Now I get it."

"No, everyone, *including* you," said Claire. "Don't be such a pain, Savoy."

"Let's go talk about it—but by the fire," Sarah said. "Now that we're not running around, I'm freezing."

Since the fire had dwindled to some smoldering yet very hot coals, Claire and I took charge of looking for some more wood. She and I split up to search. I remembered finding lots of kindling over by this small wooded area near the cove the summer before, when I was at a bonfire then. I walked carefully so I wouldn't crash into any twigs and picked up a few small fallen branches and logs.

All of a sudden I heard a voice. "Claire?" I asked softly. "That you?"

No response.

I stopped and listened again. I couldn't make out who it was, or even if it was anything besides the breeze rustling the leaves.

I got moving, quietly, stepping through the underbrush to the cove.

That's when I saw two figures standing on the sand. One of them was Jackson. He was only about ten feet away and he was facing me, but couldn't see me because of the thick overhang of trees I was standing in.

I could see him in that way you can make out a face or

figure that's really familiar to you, even on a pitch-black night. He was talking to someone—a girl. I watched for a second. I knew I probably shouldn't. But I had to know who he was with. Then they moved closer to each other and started kissing.

It was just like Claire had said: he'd dated a hundred girls since that dumb incident with me. Summer had barely begun, and here he was, hooking up with someone.

Then I looked closer. The girl was tall with long, wavy brown hair, and was wearing short plaid shorts that showed off her long, toned legs.

Jackson? Kissing *Mikayla*?

Or should I say: Mikayla, kissing Jackson?

Seriously?!?!

CHAPTER 16

Mikayla

Sometimes when I go for a hard early-morning run, it helps clear my mind, and everything that comes afterward seems relatively easy in comparison.

Not today.

I was supposed to be thinking of how to break the news to Lucy. Instead, all I could think about was Jackson and how amazing being in his arms had felt. When Sarah and Henry had dropped me off the night before, I'd run inside the house, hoping she was still up so we could talk, so everything could be out in the open.

But her door was closed and the lights were out, so I'd had to wait until morning. Instead I'd curled up on my bed and spent another hour texting with Jackson, trying to plan the next time we could get together.

I could only run through this scenario in my head so many times. *Lucy, you kind of hate Jackson. And I kind of like him—a lot, actually.* Just thinking about being with him last night almost made me weak in the knees—or maybe I'd run too fast, and too far.

I walked into the house, hoping she was up and that she'd listen to me without getting upset. She'd understand— she had to. We were best friends. We supported each other, always, no matter what was on the line.

Then again, she might tell me that I should stay away from Jackson, that he'd only end up being a jerk to me the way he had been to her. She might think that was supporting me.

Only I couldn't stay away from him. After last night, that was impossible.

So I had to make this work somehow. What was the worst that could happen? I'd tell her, and she'd be furious with me, and then I'd probably have to move out. . . . Where would I go next? I wondered. Was I really risking one of the best friendships ever for someone I'd only known for a week?

Lucy was sitting in a chair by the doorway to the back deck. "Hey. Good morning," I said.

She didn't answer at first. Then I realized she had her

headphones in and was watching something on her tablet.

I poured myself a glass of juice. I'd wait.

I sat at the counter and leafed through the local free paper someone left on our doorstep each week. This one was full of ads for events surrounding the Fourth of July, which was a week away: concerts, fireworks, a carnival, sidewalk sales, and the Bridgeport Bay 5K.

Lucy finally slipped off her headphones and came over to the refrigerator. "Hey," I said. "What are you watching?"

"Nothing much."

"Oh. Well, uh, last night was fun," I said, trying to broach the subject in a casual way. Maybe if we talked about someone else first, it would help. "Who was that guy you were talking to—the one with red hair?"

"That's Gus," Lucy said.

"Gus. Right! How do you know him?" I asked.

"He came into the store one day. He works for a caterer. It's—it's a long story," she said. "Anyway, Claire knows him too."

"Oh. That's, um, interesting," I said. "Do you like him?"

"No." Lucy shrugged. "I don't know, maybe." She nearly glared at me. This wasn't exactly the mood I wanted her to be in, but I had no choice. She was headed back to her chair.

I got up and followed her. *Now or never.* "I have to talk

to you about something," I said. "Um, I think I might have broken the handle on the bathroom sink this morning. When I went to shut it off, it turned too far and sort of got stuck there."

"It's working fine now," she said.

"Yeah? Okay, well. Phew." I laughed, uneasy. "That's a relief. I thought I broke it. Right. So that was the first thing. The second thing is . . . well, it's . . . kind of harder to say."

"What is it?" Lucy asked, looking at me.

"Do you remember when I told you and Claire about this guy I'd met at Earl Grey's, and how he nearly crashed into my bike . . . we got along really well, but I didn't know his name?"

"Sure," Lucy said.

"Well, that's Jackson," I said. "Your Jackson."

"There's no such thing as 'my' Jackson," Lucy said. "And what do you mean? You've known each other a lot longer than you said last night?"

I nodded. "I didn't tell you the whole story last night— at least, not the part about how many times I'd talked to him. Still, nothing happened between us, I mean, we were just friends, until last night when we . . . well, we kissed. I mean, who knows what will happen next, because this *just* happened." I watched Lucy's face carefully for a reaction.

I expected her to be shocked, upset—maybe furious with me. She looked completely neutral, though. "Lucy? You okay?" I asked.

"Of course I am," she said, brightening a little bit. "I'm surprised . . . I mean, I don't know if you really want to trust him after . . ."

"I *know* this is awkward and I never would have tried to find him to go after him—it's just that by the time we connected—that's when I discovered who he was, and . . ."

"And what?" Lucy asked.

"It was too late because I already liked him. As soon as I found out who he was, I knew I shouldn't talk to him, or see him that way. I tried to. But it's like . . . we just sort of, I don't know . . . click? I'm sorry."

"Why are you sorry?" Lucy asked. "It's okay if you like him, as long as he likes you. . . ."

She was acting very nonchalant. I wondered if this really didn't bother her as much as it had seemed to when we started the conversation. If she'd adjusted to the idea that quickly, I'd be surprised.

She might be faking it just to make me feel better. And that, actually, made me feel even worse.

"I mean, it's a little awkward," Lucy finally said. "I'll give you that."

"I know," I agreed. "And I don't want it to be."

"And I'm not sure you should trust him. That's a problem," Lucy said.

"I don't know—I really feel like I *can*," I said.

Suddenly, there was a loud knock on the front door, and I almost jumped, I was so startled—talking to Lucy about Jackson was making me really tense. She didn't seem to be angry, but she wasn't thrilled, either, that was for sure.

Lucy headed for the door. I hoped Jackson hadn't decided to drop by unexpectedly. This was not good timing.

CHAPTER 17

Lucy

"What's going on?" Ava asked.

She stood on the doorstep, with a large striped duffel bag at her feet. She was wearing a couple of layered tanks, khaki shorts, and sandals. Her dyed-black hair was cut at an angle so that her bangs fell across her eyes.

Mikayla and I both threw our arms around her. I couldn't have asked for a better surprise right then. If Jackson had stood on the front steps instead of Ava, I think I would have thrown up a little.

It wasn't that I disliked him, or Mikayla, obviously, but the idea of them being a couple—if that's what they truly were—did make me feel slightly ill.

On the other hand, I was relieved that Mikayla had been

up-front with me. I couldn't have endured living in the same house if she'd kept that sort of secret from me. Though I couldn't shake the feeling that she *had* been keeping a secret from me already. After all, she had known that Jackson was the guy who'd crashed into her before last night, yet she'd neglected to mention that when she told me she knew him. Maybe it wasn't outright betrayal, but it sure felt like it.

Plus, I had to worry about whether he was going to act the same way with her that he had with me. Sure, we were all a lot more grown up now. That didn't mean he wasn't capable of hurting her feelings, even unintentionally. I didn't want Jackson, of all people, to ruin Mikayla's summer.

"Sorry I'm late," Ava said. "I had to stop and ask directions to this place about ten times, because it didn't even show up on Google Maps, and—"

"Late? How can you be late when we didn't even know you were coming?" I asked. "Why are you here?"

Ava looked taken aback. "That's not much of a welcome."

"Sorry, but why aren't you in Chicago?" Mikayla added.

"Do not even talk about my internship. Do not even speak the words 'Chicago' or 'internship.'"

"Too late," Mikayla said. "What happened?"

"We can talk about it later. Are you guys going to let me in, or what?" She peered over my head to the living room and kitchen behind us.

"Sure, of course! Come on in," I said, laughing, glad for the comic relief and distraction Ava was providing. I needed to talk about something else—*with* someone else.

Ava and I dragged her duffel bag through the door and pushed it against the sofa. She deposited a slightly crumpled box of donuts and muffins on the kitchen counter. Then she collapsed into the only comfortable chair we had, looking as tired as if she'd just run a marathon. Her face was paler than usual, which is saying a lot. I quickly got her a cup of coffee, just the way she liked it, with cream, sugar, and a tiny bit of cinnamon, and set it down on the cardboard box/coffee table beside her.

"So *this* is the place that you guys were so excited about living in?" She lifted her mug and took a sip of coffee as she surveyed the room. "Needs a little work."

"I know, but we've been doing a lot," I said. "You should have seen it when we moved in."

"Seriously?" she asked. "Because I could get some fabric and make some curtains, pillows—stuff like that," Ava offered. "I think we should pick a color scheme and—"

"Wait a second. You sound like you're moving in. Are you *staying*?" Mikayla asked.

"Sure, for a while," Ava said.

"Yay!" Mikayla cried, leaning over to give her a hug. "I'm so glad."

"That's great," I said, while inside I wondered how I'd be able to pull this off. By telling my mom and grandparents, or by *not* telling them? Ava never stuck with anything for long. If she got bored or wasn't having fun, she'd move on, rather than waiting for things to change. After she quit our soccer team midseason (which I was furious about for a while), she joined the drama club. She appeared in a play and was really good at that, too—but she dropped out and took up Peace Leaders, this group that travels around working with anti-bullying initiatives in elementary schools.

My mom and my grandparents think she's too flaky, and maybe sometimes she is, but I didn't care. I really needed Ava to be here right now, considering how weird things had just gotten between me and Mikayla. "Um, for how long?" I asked.

"I'll have to see. If I find a job, then for the summer, or what's left of it. If I can't get a job, then I'll probably have to head home in a few days," she said. "I do not plan on doing that, just so you know. Because guess who would never let me live that down? Dean, of course."

Dean had been one of the reasons Ava wanted to get completely out of the Cities for the summer. Though he didn't want to date her anymore, he also didn't want to let her go. It was complicated.

"He'd be all, 'You're back—I *told* you you couldn't hack it in Chicago,'" Ava said. "And I'd be like, 'Shut up, dummy. You broke up with me, so why do you even care what I'm doing,' you know?"

I noticed she wanted to talk about anything but the reason she was here and not in Chicago working for *Faux* magazine. Still, I had to ask. "So what really did happen? Was it horrible?"

"You've seen disaster movies, right?" She smiled. "Like that. So do you think I can crash here for a few days?"

"You can sleep in my room," Mikayla said. "There are actually twin beds. They're kind of on the firm side, and a little bit short, but they're not horrible."

"They sound like cots," Ava said. "But I could sleep on the floor, I'm so beat."

I knew Ava wanted to crash for a while, but I couldn't wait to tell her what was going on. I hadn't even told Claire that I'd seen Jackson and Mikayla together—I was so shocked and confused that I'd ditched the hunt for firewood and gone home. Maybe that was childish, but I didn't know what else to do.

"This is so relaxing. I love it. I can't believe you guys have your own place." Ava leaned back and stretched her arms above her head. "So why don't *you* guys seem relaxed?"

"What? We're relaxed," Mikayla said.

"Sure. I was just watching a movie. Totally chilling," I added.

Ava looked at me. "I still say you're not acting like yourselves."

"You haven't seen us in two weeks. We've changed. Totally changed," I joked.

"Riiiiiiight. So do you know of anyone who's hiring?" she asked.

Mikayla grabbed a couple of muffins from the box on the counter and brought them over on a plate. "I don't think we're hiring at the Club, but I'll ask. With so many shops around there has to be something." She set the plate on the table. "Thanks for the breakfast, Ava."

"No problem," Ava said. "I felt like I had to buy something since I was asking for directions. And you know what? They're actually pretty good. Try one."

"Thanks." I took a mini chocolate-chip muffin. "The problem is that you're getting here a couple weeks late." I drummed my fingers on the arm of the folding chair. "But who knows? Maybe someone's busier than they thought. It's been a little slow for us so far, but my nana keeps saying it's totally normal. It's the first week of July when the place goes nuts."

"Then I say I got here just in time," Ava said, pulling the top off a banana muffin.

"Where do you *want* to work?" Mikayla asked her. "And what about your mom? Does she think it's okay if you stay here instead of Chicago?"

"She's totally fine with it. She was worried about me being on my own anyway. So now that I'm here . . . she knows I'll be safe. As for what kind of job I get? I really don't care," Ava said. "I can wait tables, fold T-shirts, make lattes—I have all kinds of experience."

Mikayla laughed. "Yeah, because you quit every place after a month!"

Ava smiled. "Maybe, but that means I have tons of different skills. So it's actually a good thing. I'm experienced."

"I wouldn't go around saying that. Might give people the wrong idea," I said.

"Or the right idea," Mikayla teased her.

"Shut up!" Ava tossed a pillow at her then, turning to me, she asked, "How's your job going? I got your messages about working with Jackson. Remind me again who he is? You guys made out a couple of years ago or what?"

"No!" I practically yelled. "We kissed once. Look, it's no

big deal." I shook my head. I did *not* want to talk about that now. It made me feel so dumb, so juvenile. "Let's move on."

"Well, you know the old saying. Kiss me once, shame on you, kiss me twice . . . you know, good for me," Ava said.

I squirmed uncomfortably on the sofa. I didn't want to talk about this right now. I might say something I'd regret. This whole situation was so dramatic all of a sudden. I didn't want it to be, not this way.

"I think it's '*Fool* me once, shame on you,'" Mikayla said, laughing.

"Whatever," Ava said. "I have my sayings, you have yours. So what's the deal with him, anyway?"

"It's not—look, things have changed." I glanced at Mikayla. Who exactly was supposed to be sharing this news, anyway? *Me?* "Why don't you tell her?"

"Tell her?" she repeated, as if she were completely not part of the conversation.

"You guys are acting weird. This is like the time you refused to tell me I had spinach in my teeth after I auditioned for the spring play. Tell me already," Ava demanded.

"Mikayla's got a boyfriend," I blurted out.

"Hold on a second. Hold on. This is monumental news. I'm—I'm shocked. No, I'm making mimosas." Ava jumped out of the chair.

"We don't have champagne. What do you think this is, a hotel?"

Ava peered inside the fridge. "You've got orange juice and Sprite. Close enough. So who's the guy?" She pulled three glasses—our only three glasses—out of the cupboard and started pouring.

Mikayla slowly untied her running shoes. She took her time. She was stalling, waiting for me to jump in, but it was her news. She could feel bad about sharing it—I know I would. It was like she'd deliberately chosen Jackson, which was so strange. There were lots of guys here, but she'd ended up with the one I had been avoiding for years.

"It's Jackson," Mikayla finally said.

Ava looked at Mikayla, then at me, then at Mikayla. "Are you making this up?"

We both shook our heads.

"Um, guys. This is not the way to start the summer." Ava stirred our fake mimosas with a spoon. She looked over at me. "I mean, how do you feel about it?"

Good question, I thought, just as my phone rang. I glanced at it and saw my mom's number. "Hold that thought," I said to Ava. "I have to get this." Truth be told, I kind of needed my mom right then. I grabbed the mimosa and ducked into my bedroom, closing the door behind me.

"The wedding's off," Mom said, when I answered. "It's completely and totally off."

"What? You're not getting married? Why not?"

"Oh, we're getting married all right," she said. "Just *not* at the Hiawatha Country Club. Don't get me started."

"I didn't," I said quietly. But I had a feeling it wouldn't matter.

"They double-booked us, Luce. Double-booked *us*," she complained, as if I hadn't heard her the first time. "What a bunch of amateurs! Have you ever heard of something so unbelievably incompetent?"

"Um . . ."

"Well, have you?" she asked.

"I'm not sure. I guess—"

"Now how am I going to find a decent place to have a wedding in August? The date is less than two months away and the absolute height of wedding season," she went on.

I thought June was the height—June brides and all that—but I decided not to bring that up at the moment.

"We won't be able to get it in the paper—well, thank goodness the invitations didn't go out yet, but they're already printed. I have to rethink *everything*."

Funny how Mom could make it sound as if she was trying to negotiate a truce in the Middle East, when all she was talking about was switching a location. With two months' notice to do so, and it was her second marriage, not her first, and she was supposed to be a grown-up. Sometimes she seemed like the youngest grown-up I'd ever met.

"Mom, there's another way to approach this," I said. She wouldn't take my advice, but I was going to plow ahead and give it anyway. "Why not just have a, um, more simple wedding? That would mean you could find a smaller place and—"

"What? Lucy, come on. I don't do things on a small scale. You know me. This is one of the most important days of my life! Gary has already revoked his country club membership, which is really too bad because the club is a good source for realtors, but we had to take a stand. I have to scramble to find a halfway decent place with a large outdoor patio. Are you *sure* you can't come home for a week or so and help me straighten this mess out?"

As much as I didn't want to get roped into the wedding plans, I was almost tempted for a second. It wouldn't be fun, exactly, but it might be better than trying to deal with the current weird situation in this little house. "I can't, Mom. Nana and Grandpa need me here," I said.

"I suppose they do need you." She let out a deep sigh. "So what's new there?" she finally asked.

I wanted to tell her everything: about Ava showing up,

about having to work with Jackson after he'd humiliated me three years ago, about discovering Jackson and Mikayla together the night before. It was going to take a few days to stop feeling so blindsided. "Mom," I said. "Have you ever had a friendship get really weird all of a sudden?"

"Well . . . sure," she said. "I guess, over time. Friendships can change when people grow and change. But you make it sound like more of an emergency than that. What's the issue? I assume you're talking about Mikayla."

"It's just . . . I really trusted her. With everything," I said. "And now, I'm not sure that I can."

"What happened?"

"You know what, never mind," I said. "I bet it will blow over and I'll feel stupid for even asking the question."

"Lucyloo. Whenever you don't want to talk . . . it usually means there's something to talk about," Mom said.

She was right. When she and my dad told me they were getting separated, I didn't tell them how I felt for weeks. I was so shocked and so angry with them for not saying anything until the day Dad was moving out—they'd never told me this was even being discussed. And then, *wham*. Guess what? Dad's moving out.

I was starting to get mad at Mikayla just for reminding me of all these awful feelings. This was the last thing I wanted to think about on my summer vacation. This was the time I could get away from it all.

But, funny thing: you couldn't actually get away from things like that, not when your best friend had kind of broken your trust too. She didn't tell me she knew him until she had to. The fact they were making out a couple of hours later meant they'd had time enough together to get close. Without telling me.

"Honey, don't worry. You'll work things out. You've been close friends too long to let something come between you," Mom said. "Oops—Gary's on the other line, talk to you later!"

After I hung up, I glanced into the living room, where Ava was sitting. I didn't see Mikayla anywhere, so I tentatively walked back out. As I passed the bathroom, I heard the shower running and figured she must have ducked in. I hoped she hadn't heard me talking about her.

"Mikayla had to get ready for work," Ava told me as I sat down opposite her. "Which is good, because you and I will have a chance to talk."

"I have to leave pretty soon too," I said, then sipped the orange juice and Sprite.

"Yes. But not right this second. Because I gotta ask you— is this going to be weird or what?"

"What?" I brushed at a muffin crumb on the table beside me.

"What? Like you don't know? Give me a break. Luce, I saw your face earlier. The Mikayla and Jackson hookup! Is that okay with you? For real?" Ava demanded.

I didn't know what to say. I'd never lie to Ava, but she'd just gotten here. I didn't want her to land right in the middle of a controversy. "It's weird. But it's okay with me. I mean, I don't like him anymore."

"Not at all?"

"Not like that," I said. "It's been years. It was super awkward at first, but we're starting to act like normal people around each other, so, I mean, that's an improvement. I never wanted to see him . . . *see* him."

"Yeah, but still. It has to be strange," Ava said.

"It will be, when I see him at work next time," I said. "She didn't know who he was . . . at least, that's what she said. I mean, she didn't know he was the same Jackson. I'm guessing he didn't know she was my roommate and friend, either, or he would have said something." I tried to imagine the timeline, and how they'd managed to spend time hanging out without me having a clue. I guess I'd been busy too. We were sort of doing our own things, in some ways, this summer—that had its upsides and its downsides. "I know it's not the end of the world or anything, but it's just kind of . . . ew. You know?"

I looked over at Ava. She was asleep.

Great. Now I had no one to talk to about it—except Mikayla, who had just opened the bathroom door after her shower. I waited for her to go down the hall and close her bedroom door. Then I hurried to my room, grabbed my bathrobe, and slipped into the bathroom for a hot shower. I could stay in here awhile, until she either left for work or gave up on me. Sure, that was ignoring the problem. But for this morning, I'd had more honest conversations than I could take. I needed a break.

CHAPTER 18

Mikayla

Tuesday afternoon, my phone chimed with a new text and I pulled it out of my pocket to glance at it.

Can't stop thinking about you.

Same here, I wrote back.

Jackson and I hadn't gotten together the night before because it was Ava's first night in town and Ava, Lucy, and I had gone out. As happy as I was to spend time with Ava, I was dying to see Jackson again. The past thirty-six hours had felt like an eternity.

We'd talked a lot on the phone and I'd found out more about him, from his favorite foods (chips, salsa, and guac) to his college ideas (West Coast, East Coast, something with a coast) to his first concert, his hangouts back home, his best vacation, and on and on. We had a lot in common when it came to music and sports—we didn't play the same exact ones, but we were competitive and we both started on varsity. We talked about what we'd do with athletic scholarships and how we balanced team responsibilities with homework. At home, he worked at Lunds, but not at the location where my family usually went. Still, it was weird to think that we'd probably walked by each other before without noticing.

Talking and texting was nice, but it wasn't the same as being with him. I needed that. As hard as it was to admit to Lucy, and Ava, and even myself—I had already fallen for Jackson, to the point where there was no going back. I really hoped that Lucy wouldn't ask me to.

When can I see you? Jackson wrote.

After 5? I texted back.

Can't wait that long. Just quit your job already.

Ha ha, I wrote back. *You first!*

If it meant I could be with you all day, I would.

"Miss Mikayla, you promised me you'd show me how to stop getting ten-offs."

I looked up from my phone screen. Jeremy, one of the campers I was supposed to be looking after, was standing in front of me. I slid my phone into my pocket, blushing. "Sorry about that. Just a small emergency." A boyfriend emergency. Was there such a thing? How would I know? *Boyfriend.* It had never felt right to put that word together with me before.

"Do you have to leave?" Jeremy asked.

"Oh, no. It's fine," I said.

"'Cause if you have to, that's fine. My mom's a surgeon and she's constantly leaving when she gets those kinds of texts that make her look like she's kind of freaking out," he said.

"Trust me," I said. "It wasn't that serious, even if I did look freaked out." I laughed, feeling embarrassed. "I have a long way to go to be as important as your mom. What kind of medicine is she in?"

"She does a lot of those appendix things," Jeremy said.

"Ah. Have you ever had to have your appendix out?" I asked.

"No way. And I'm not going to." He shook his head. "I broke my leg when I was little and that was horrible."

He said "when I was little" like it was a long time ago. At most, he was about nine years old. I couldn't remember his age exactly. "How old were you?" I asked.

"Four?" he said. "I was trying to learn how to jump off a slide. On my brother's skateboard. Have you ever broken your leg?" Jeremy asked.

"Nope. I broke my arm once, though," I said. "Playing softball."

"What about that scar on your leg?" Jeremy pointed at my shin. "What's that from?"

"Oh, that? That's nothing. I fell on my bike, that's all," I felt my face turn hot at the memory. If I hadn't nearly gotten run over by Jackson's car, I might never have met him. Or if I did, I'd have met him at the Apple Store, with Lucy beside me, and I'd probably have never given him a chance.

But then I wouldn't be in the predicament I was in right now. When I'd left for work that morning, she and Ava were laughing and talking and she didn't seem bothered in the slightest by my news. But it was hard to get a read on her sometimes.

Should I talk to her again about whether it bugged her or not?

Should I not see Jackson until I was sure?

"Um, Miss Mikayla? You were going to teach me how to not get ten-offs, remember?" Jeremy reminded me.

"Right. Right! Okay, so here's what we do." I'd only learned shuffleboard a few days ago, but I was quickly getting the hang of it. "There's no surefire way to avoid them. But I can teach you some things that will make you better overall. Come on, grab a cue."

Another text chimed on my phone. *Come see me at work.*

I can't, I wrote. *Can't get away.*

Me either, he wrote back. *When are you done?*

"If you have to go, it's okay," Jeremy said. "I can practice by myself."

"No. It's not okay. I'm here to work." As much as I didn't want to, I switched off my phone. It was killing me not to be able to see Jackson right away, but this was work. I needed to see him, but I also needed this job. "Let's play another game." I started lining up the disks. "This time, let's see how many sevens we can score."

"Probably zero," he said.

"What? Come on, Jeremy, I know you can do better than that." I stepped back and looked at him, with his shuffle-board cue over his shoulder. "I bet you can get two. And if you don't? You have to buy me a waffle cone."

"Those are, like, eight bucks," he complained.

"Exactly. So get two sevens to save eight bucks," I said. "And if you do, then I'll buy you one."

"That math is really messed up." He started lining up the disks. "If you get me in ten-off, then what do I get?"

"More lessons," I said. "And less math."

He nodded. "Deal."

I was putting all the croquet mallets, balls, and wickets into a long wooden locker when I suddenly felt someone touching my back. I turned, expecting to see one of the many kids coming to get me, but instead saw Jackson standing behind me. "Oh my gosh, you scared me." I laughed and put my hand over my mouth.

"Sorry." Jackson put his arms around my waist. "I just . . . you know. I had to see you."

"Yeah. I know what you mean," I said, putting my hands on his shoulders.

He pulled me closer and kissed my cheek, then my neck, then his lips were brushing lightly against mine. It was kind of like torture. In a good way.

"I saw you just now," Jackson said. "Playing croquet."

"You did?"

"You're so good with kids. I'm impressed. How many younger brothers and sisters do you have, again?"

"Three," I said. "And then there are the cousins who live with us sometimes. And the dog, the cat—"

"Good old Cinnamon," Jackson teased. "Sounds like a full house."

"You have no idea," I said.

"Yeah, I'll have to see that." Jackson smiled.

There was this awkward pause. He looked at me kind of bashfully and I stared at the ground. We'd only been whatever it was we were for a few days, since the night of the bonfire.

Who knew if we'd even last out the week, never mind the summer. And after that? What should I say?

"You want to get something to eat?" he asked.

"Dying to," I said, relieved that he'd changed the subject. "Give me ten minutes?"

I hurried inside the Club's main building to sign out of work and quickly change into some nonwork clothes. We'd talked about getting together after work, so I'd packed a skirt and tank and sandals.

Jackson was waiting outside in the parking lot, beside his car. "Where to?" he asked, opening the door for me.

"I don't know," I said. "You know the area a lot better than I do. Should we get takeout and go somewhere, or eat at the Blackbird, or—"

"I have an idea," Jackson said as we drove through town. "There's this old diner over in Avonville. They have great Juicy Lucys and it's a pretty cool place."

A Juicy Lucy is a cheeseburger where the cheese is cooked inside the burger—Minneapolis and Saint Paul have a bunch of restaurants that compete to offer the tastiest one. It was a food that Lucy hated—just because of the name.

Lucy, I thought. I had to tell Jackson I lived with Lucy. . . . I had to tell him that things might be a little weird for a while, because even though she claimed it wasn't a big deal—it *was* a big deal. The reaction on her face had told me that. We'd been friends long enough for me to know when she was faking her feelings. This was one of those times.

In fact, I probably ought to be heading to the cabin to hang out with her and talk things over some more, instead of riding out of town with Jackson.

"So I was thinking about something on my way over here. I don't even know where you live," Jackson said. "That's weird. Why don't I know?"

"It hasn't really come up yet?" I said. If I told Jackson I lived with Lucy, would it change the way he felt about me? I didn't have much choice, though. Maybe clearing the air with him would help make things better all around.

"Well, this is going to sound kind of weird, but I live in a small house on Hemlock Hill Road. And I actually live with someone you know. Lucy. Lucy Carpenter?" I said timidly.

"Oh, yeah—I saw you guys sitting next to each other at the bonfire. But—roommates? I mean, you know we work together, right? Why didn't either of you tell me?" Jackson asked.

"At first I didn't know who you *were*. I mean, I sort of fell for you before I even knew you guys had this connection from growing up—"

"Wait a second, wait a second," Jackson said. "You fell for

me?" He reached over and interlaced his fingers with mine.

"I met you and I was spending time with you, but I didn't know your name. Then when I found out—well, I didn't tell her right away," I explained.

"Why not? And why didn't *she* tell me you guys lived together?" He looked confused.

"It never came up between you?" I said. "I meant to tell you once I knew who you were and that you guys worked together, and I was going to, but—I don't know. You and Lucy have this history."

"History? What history? We were friends once." Jackson shrugged. "We had a falling-out or whatever you call it."

"Because . . . ," I prompted.

"I don't know. Something happened," Jackson said.

"Something? Don't you know what it was?" I wanted to hear his side of the story.

"Not really," he said. "I guess—well, maybe she sort of had a crush on me, which I can't really believe now. We went through some awkward phase, but that was middle school. I mean, seriously. Big drama over nothing. Then we moved and I switched schools—didn't she switch schools too?"

"Yeah, you kind of *have* to when middle school's over," I teased him.

"Ha ha. Anyway, she and I are perfectly fine, as long as

you and I are," Jackson said. "If anything, I think it's cool that we have this connection. It's like Lucy introduced us. Only she didn't." When he put it like that, it sounded right. Like it made sense.

But it isn't really like that, I thought. *Not at all.* Lucy might be saying she was okay with it—and she even might be, but I doubted she would have wished it or planned it. She'd have been much happier if she never saw Jackson again, or if she had a completely different coworker for the summer.

I was going to have to work on making this okay for her. The last thing I wanted, seriously, was for Lucy to have a bad summer while I was having the best one of my life. In fact, it actually couldn't be the best summer for me, if she and I couldn't be close friends the way we'd been the past three years. That would ruin it, Jackson or no.

One step at a time, I thought, remembering the advice my dad usually gave me when I would freak out about everything going right for a certain event, or game, or meet. Best foot forward. I'd work things out with her.

After Jackson parked and before we got out of the car, he pulled me closer to him. Our lips met in one of those devastating kisses you see in movies; it felt like everything in the world was riding on this one kiss.

At least that's how it felt to me.

We separated for a moment, and his hand caressed my cheek. "I haven't, like, actually done this before. But . . . do you want to go out?"

"I thought we were," I said, looking into his eyes. "You mean . . . tomorrow? Again?" I tried to remember what was already on my calendar, if I had something planned with Lucy. Maybe I should spend the night hanging out with her and Ava.

"No. Well, maybe," he said. "I actually meant—go out. Like, exclusively."

"As in . . ." I wanted to be sure I had it right, that I knew what he was asking. I'd wondered before if this was what I should call him—if we were at that point yet.

"Boyfriend, girlfriend," Jackson said. "Me, you."

"Um, sure." I nodded. "I mean, yes!" I smiled so widely that my face kind of hurt.

"You're a mess sometimes. A hot mess, but still." He curled my hair behind my ears and we started kissing again. I had a feeling we wouldn't be going into the diner anytime soon.

CHAPTER 19

Lucy

Ava and I climbed into my car just as Mikayla rode off on her bike to work at the Club Thursday morning. I felt relieved when Mikayla left, because every time I was around her the past couple of days, I was really uncomfortable. I was beginning to wonder if it would ever get any better or feel any more normal that she and Jackson were seeing each other.

"I should get a bike, probably," Ava said as she watched Mikayla disappear down the road. "I think my car is going to last about two more miles and that's it." She looked over at her small Subaru, which was about twenty years old.

"We can definitely find a good used bike for you around here," I said to Ava. "There's a shop on Bay Street that sells old rentals. I mean, if it comes to that."

"What do you mean if it comes to that?" Ava asked.

"Well, we're not even sure you're staying—I mean, it depends whether you get a job," I said.

"I'll find one, no problem," Ava said confidently. "Or have you forgotten that I have lots of experience waiting tables? Too much experience, actually."

"You're right. Of course you'll get a job." Sure, Bridgeport was a busy community and getting a summer job was competitive—and difficult at the last minute. But Ava had this way of charming people.

"So, this club Mikayla works at. What's it called again?" asked Ava.

"Bridgeport Beach Club," I said.

"And are we members there?" she asked.

"*We?* You just got here. And no. And neither are my grandparents, in case that was your next question."

"Why not? You're saying we can't even *go* there?" Ava demanded.

I shook my head. "Not unless we pay their ridiculous dues."

"But we can sneak in," Ava said. "There's no law against that."

"Um . . . I think there is," I said. "That's why it's called *sneaking*? I wouldn't try it. Everything in this place gets back to people, one way or another."

"Hm. I think I can avoid getting caught. That is, as long as it's worth the risk. "

"What are you, a jewel thief all of a sudden?" I teased her. "How about we don't break any rules this summer?"

"Why not? You need to loosen up, take a few risks. Wasn't that one of your goals for the summer? Learning how to take risks?"

"Yeah, maybe," I admitted. I tapped my fingers against the door as I rested my arm on the open window. "I'm not sure how well that's working out for me."

"Really, why's that?" asked Ava.

"Things have been kind of dicey lately," I began. "Around the house. Well, really anytime Mikayla and I are in the same room. I said I was okay with her and Jackson hooking up . . . but I don't think I am."

"All I can say is the tension between you guys is killing me. It's like as high as that freaking wall we had to scale on that dumb obstacle course when we were in the Turtle Pod."

"You kept yelling, 'Turtles don't scale walls! Turtles don't scale walls!'" I laughed, remembering the look on her fourteen-year-old face.

"Meanwhile, Mikayla scaled the thing in like two

seconds. And I was lying on the ground with rope burn."
Ava rolled her eyes. "If I ever sign up for something called
orientation again, remind me not to. So, I've felt the tension
too. But you told her you were okay with it, so are you or
aren't you?"

I should have known I couldn't hide it from Ava. I
breathed in and let it out slowly. "I've been trying to keep it
all to myself, hoping that I'll feel better about things, but it
just isn't working. You're right."

"Why didn't you talk to me earlier?" Ava asked. "I've been
around."

"I know, but I was trying to deal with it on my own. Turns
out, I just get angrier," I admitted. "I just—I can't believe that
about two seconds after she told me she knew him, they were
making out on the beach."

"What do you mean? What beach?" asked Ava.

The image of Jackson and Mikayla making out on the
beach flashed through my mind. "Don't tell Mikayla, but I
saw them together—and it looked pretty serious—and that
was before she told me anything about their connection. That
means she knew him a lot better and a lot longer than she's
really letting on. And why would she do that when she knows
how much he hurt me? They meet—without telling me—
and start some kind of, like, relationship, before I am even

clued in to the fact they know each other. I mean, why didn't she say how she met him? Why didn't she mention it *before* the bonfire—or when she finally told me at the bonfire she sort of knew him, why didn't she go into detail and tell me she really, really liked him?"

"I don't know, because I wasn't there. Why don't you ask her?" Ava said gently.

"I don't know . . . because I can't," I said.

"Why not? It's an honest question," Ava said. "I bet she'd rather know how you're really feeling than have you fake being happy about it. You guys can talk about it—"

"But what if that doesn't work?" I said.

"Is *not* talking working?" Ava countered.

I sighed, frustrated. "I want to be happy for her. But it seems like she didn't put much thought into all this. She should have known how difficult this could be for me."

"She does know, I think. And come on, when you fall for someone—it doesn't involve a whole lot of thinking. Sometimes you're not a hundred percent rational."

"True. The thing is—ugh. Couldn't it be anyone *else*?" I heard a siren and glanced in the rearview mirror. A police car was coming up fast behind me. I pulled over to the shoulder to let it go past. Instead, it pulled over behind *me*, lights flashing.

"Oh, great. Now what?" I asked Ava.

"You *were* going kind of fast. Some turtle you've turned out to be."

I laughed, despite the situation. I got out my license and registration for the officer, who was approaching the car. "You don't understand. You get parking tickets all the time, but the thing is *I* don't get tickets. Ever. As a rule."

"Things are going to get better. Trust me. Mikayla would not want you to feel so bad about this. Anyway, we're turtles. We have to stick together," Ava said. "Otherwise we get killed by coyotes."

"Thanks," I told her.

"For what?"

"Talking about it with me." I leaned over to give her a quick hug. "Even though I didn't want to talk about it, at first. It helped."

The officer rapped on the window. "Excuse me, girls, do you mind? License and registration, please."

"Sorry, officer," Ava spoke up. "I was just consoling her. It's the first time she's ever been pulled over. Ever. She's the best driver I know."

The officer did not look amused.

"Here you go, sir." I handed over my license.

* * *

"You're late," Jackson said when I walked in the back door of the store.

"I know. I got a speeding ticket," I said. "How dumb can I be?"

I wouldn't mention that maybe the reason I was speeding was because I was talking about Mikayla dating him and how upsetting that was. It wasn't his fault. Exactly. But had he not been a jerk to me three years ago, this whole thing wouldn't be an issue at all.

Anyway, I was going to make every attempt to steer the conversation away from that, Mikayla, and anything not related to apples.

"You got a ticket?" Jackson's eyebrows shot up.

"Yes, me. What's so surprising about that?"

"You just don't—I don't know. Do you speed a lot?"

"No. Never," I said.

"Well." He coughed. "Not *never*," he corrected me.

"Ha ha." I glared at him. "Very funny."

"Sorry," he said. "That sucks. I hate getting tickets. I mean, I've only had parking tickets so far. One time I failed to yield, but the cop gave me a warning instead of a ticket."

"Failure to yield. I think I saw that movie," I said. "I was talking to Ava and I got carried away."

"Who's Ava? Oh, wait—is she your other roommate? I

think maybe Mikayla mentioned her showing up," Jackson said. "You know, even though I met Mikayla a couple weeks ago, I didn't find out she was your roommate until recently. Why didn't you tell me?" He looked genuinely concerned.

So much for keeping the conversation away from Mikayla. Fail. "I . . . didn't know you knew her," I said with a shrug. "It didn't come up because she didn't know what you looked like or your name and . . ."

"Kind of sounds like a Shakespeare plot," Jackson said.

"Showoff," I teased him. "What, have you been studying while it's slow?" I poked at the fat book on the counter: *Ace the ACT.*

"Yeah, I have to, I'm still bad at standardized tests. Anyway, I hope it's not, like, too strange. Us hanging out."

"Why would it be strange? It's not strange." Why was he acting so concerned about my feelings? Had Mikayla told him to be?

Ew. I hated the thought of the two of them discussing me. I had to change the subject—quickly. "I have a random question," I said. "Are you doing any college tours this summer? I want to do a few and I'm wondering how to work it out with this schedule."

He looked relieved to be changing the subject too. "I'm pretty sure I know where I want to go for college," he said.

"But I don't think I'll get in, so I have to apply to like ten other places to make sure I have a good backup."

"So what's your first choice, the U?" I asked.

"No." He shook his head. "Definitely not the U."

"Carleton? Hamline? St. Thomas?" I asked, naming several private colleges in the Twin Cities area. For some reason it was easier to talk with Jackson than it was to spend time with Mikayla. Maybe because I had no choice *but* to spend eight hours a day with him—or maybe because he wasn't one of my closest friends and therefore held to a higher standard, as the saying goes.

"I was thinking more like UCLA, Stanford, Cal Tech," he said.

"Cali*fornia*?" I said. "You're going to move to California?"

"Well . . . maybe. Why? What's wrong with that?"

"No, nothing!" I felt embarrassed for how strongly I'd reacted. He probably thought that the idea of leaving the Midwest made me tremble with fear. "I'm just surprised, that's all."

He nodded. "My parents were too. I don't think they like the idea of me going so far away, but I'm going to apply anyway. Who knows, maybe I'll get in."

"California. Huh. I hadn't really considered that. I mean, not that I'm going to consider it now because you said that, but . . . maybe I've been thinking of staying too close to home. I should look around more."

"I'm kind of anxious to get away from home," Jackson said. "You remember Franklin, right?"

"Of course." I'd never really been friends with Jackson's older brother—he was way too cool to ever talk to someone like me back then. Franklin was the kind of person who ruled the hallways at school; he was a great athlete, cocaptain of the football team, and things like that. When we were little, Jackson used to want to be just like him.

"Did I tell you he's here this summer too?"

"No. He's in Bridgeport? I haven't seen him around. Where has he been hiding? Where's he working?"

"He's not," Jackson said. "He's here with my grandparents because he sort of got in with the wrong crowd at school. High school and then college," Jackson said. "He started partying too much. First it was drinking, then he got into other stuff. It's kind of been a nightmare."

"I had no idea," I said. "I'm sorry."

"Yeah. He's struggling. Like, he'll seem totally fine. Then you find out he's not. I wouldn't mind skipping the drama. So are you going to apply to the U?" Jackson asked.

"Not necessarily. I've got a top ten list—the college counselor at school said to make one over the summer. The problem is that right now I only have four schools on it."

"We should compare lists. I can help you get to ten," Jackson said.

"Seriously?" I asked. He'd really do that for me? As I was standing there feeling stunned, the door opened behind me.

"Let me guess. Northern Spy crisis?" Jackson said.

I turned to see Gus standing by the front door. "No! Actually." His face turned a bit red. "I was just walking by. I have to go to Bartholomew's Imports down the block and get some fresh spices. What are you guys up to?" he asked.

"Dusting." I held up the bright-red feather duster we had to use—the one that made us both look a little bit too much like maids.

"I didn't know apples *got* dusty," said Gus, making a face.

"They might not, but the ten thousand other items in here do. It's the Original Apple Store. We are technically required, by law, to stock every single apple souvenir item available," I said.

"Okay, if that's true, when are you going to start selling iPads?" Gus asked.

I laughed. "Wouldn't that be nice? Especially if we got our employee discount . . ."

"We have an employee discount?" asked Jackson.

"Yeah, but look around. What would you want to spend

it on?" Our inventory was geared to tourists, and middle-aged female tourists at that; those obsessed with apple pies and baking pies in general; apple fanatics; and people who loved apple magnets, calendars, and prints. That might be all one big category, come to think of it.

"Hey, can I ask you something? Where do you go to school?" Jackson suddenly asked Gus. "Are you in chef school or something?"

"Cooking school, you mean?" Gus asked. "Hardly. No, this chef gig is just a summer thing. If he yells at me much more, it might be a half-a-summer thing. In fact I'm waiting to hear about an opening at one of the kayak places."

"So are you in college?" Jackson asked him.

Gus shook his head. "I wish. No. I just finished my junior year of high school."

"He goes to school with Claire," I explained. "Right here at Bridgeport High."

"Yeah. It's more glamorous than it sounds," Gus said.

"But where do you want to go to college?" Jackson asked. "We're having a debate about whether to go far from home, or not."

"Ah! Well, living here, I don't have a lot of choice. I mean, I'm going to have to move somewhere," Gus said. "Unless I do the online option, but I'd rather be on a real campus, with other real people. Besides, I've been here my whole life."

So why hadn't Nana and Grandpa hired him? I wondered. Nothing against Jackson, but things would be a lot *less* awkward right now without him here.

"So does that mean you've had enough, um, apples for one lifetime?" I asked.

"No!" Gus cried, slamming his fists against the counter. "There are never enough apples!" he said in a heavy Russian-type accent. Then he grabbed three apples and started juggling them. Naturally, Jackson had to compete, so soon both of them were tossing apples in the air.

My phone buzzed, so I slid it out of my back pocket to check messages.

JUST got a job, Ava had texted. *I start tonight. How's it going? Cool down yet?*

I smiled as I began to write her back. The summer was definitely getting more interesting, but not in the way I'd imagined. Nothing was working out the way I'd thought it would—nothing at all. Some of it was awful. Some of it was a big question mark.

I wondered if Gus really needed spices or not. He certainly wasn't in a hurry to leave. Was he only here to hang out with us? Or . . . with me? I looked up and he was now leaning his elbows on the counter, waiting for me to stop texting.

"So," he said. "When's the next bonfire?"

"Beats me," I said. "Why don't we, um, exchange numbers. If you hear of something, let me know—and vice versa?"

We both held up our phones so that they touched. Gus's made a cute beeping sound as it captured my number, and mine responded with a *bloop*.

"Phone love," Gus commented, raising his eyebrows. "I think they really like each other."

I looked at him and smiled. If only it was that easy to tell with *people*.

CHAPTER 20

Mikayla

"Guess what? I got a job! I'm staying in town!"

"You got a job? Where?" I asked Ava. "And how did you get past the gate?"

"Oh, I didn't go through the gate. I mean, I tried, but some grumpy dude told me I needed a pass, so I found an alternate way," Ava said. "So anyway, I'm working at the Blackbird Café, starting tonight."

"Are you waiting tables?"

"Hosting and waiting tables, depending on what they need. I have to go back for training this afternoon and then work tonight," Ava said. "You'll come visit me, right?"

"Of course!"

"They said the tips are really good. And the manager is super friendly. So come on. I've got Lucy's car. She doesn't need it while she's at work. I'm here to take you to a celebration lunch," Ava said.

"I usually eat here—" I protested.

"But you're dying for a change, right? You need to get away for a break," Ava urged.

"Kind of," I admitted.

"Come on, let's grab some sandwiches and sit down on the dock, watch the ferry come in. It'll be fun."

I couldn't argue with that. Plus, I was looking forward to some time alone with Ava, so we could talk. I checked in with Sarah, who gave me permission to take off for an hour, and Ava and I zipped toward the main part of town. We parked in the ferry lot and walked to a sandwich shop.

Suddenly a red minivan pulled up beside us. A woman with curly black hair leaned out and asked, "Excuse me, but I'm looking for the Original Apple Store. Do you happen to know where it is?"

"You're going the wrong way," I said. "It's right back up that hill there." I quickly gave her directions, then Ava and I continued on our walk.

"I was just there," Ava announced as we went into the deli.

"You were?" I asked as I studied the menu, written in colorful chalk on a blackboard hanging behind the counter.

"Of course. I went in to tell Lucy about the job and ask if I could keep her car a bit longer. Yikes! You know what I just thought of? I need more white shirts and black skirts. For waitressing, I mean. I'll have to figure out where to get those this afternoon. Anyway, I have to say—Jackson is totally cute. No, more like . . . handsome cute," she said.

I turned from studying the menu board. "I know, right?" We both ordered our sandwiches and grabbed empty cups by the pop machine.

"You're lucky. Well, not that looks are everything. They're not," Ava said.

"I know," I said.

"Because I've been wondering about something. If Jackson was a jerk to Lucy, how do we know he won't suddenly start acting like that toward you?" asked Ava.

I thought it over for a minute while I filled my cup with root beer. As much as I knew about Jackson, I couldn't say for certain that he wouldn't do something like that. It was the kind of thing boys did, right? All the time, according to some of my friends.

There was the Jackson that Lucy knew, though, and the Jackson I knew: the Jackson who brought me Junior Mints after learning they were my favorite movie snack; who sent me sweet messages; who kissed me on that one spot by my ear that made me practically melt . . .

"Mikayla, stop! You're causing a flood!" Ava cried.

The root beer had spilled over the top of my cup and was running over my hands and onto the counter. I pulled my thumb away from the dispenser button and grabbed some napkins to clean up the mess.

"Did you fall asleep or what?" Ava asked as we grabbed our subs.

"I'm having a klutzy summer," I said with a nervous laugh. "This is not even the worst of it." I showed her the slight bike-crash scar on my forehead and the volleyball-induced bump on my nose, and then finished wiping up the spilled soda. I grabbed a straw and we walked out of the shop, heading to some wooden picnic tables down on the dock.

The bottoms of my sneakers were sticky from the root beer fiasco and made a funny noise as we walked on the sidewalk. We walked down the sloping hill toward the wooden dock. Tourists were lined up outside various boat slips, waiting for their tours, milling around bait shops, T-shirt shops, and the ice cream stand. There was a whole other life in Bridgeport that I didn't see much of, being stuck at the Club all day.

I shouldn't say "stuck," though. I got to work with tons of

great kids, got to be outside most of the time, and had access to everything you could ever want or need. Well, except a certain person.

Ava and I found an empty bench and settled onto it. "So *before* you flooded the sandwich place, we were talking about Jackson." Ava unwrapped her straw and pierced the top of the cup lid with it.

"Right. So I know he was a jerk to Lucy when he was younger. But he wouldn't do that now, to me. We wouldn't do that to each other. We have a real, you know, connection."

"Connection is one thing. Sticking with it? And loyalty? That's something else," Ava declared.

"Right, of course. But I mean, I don't see any reason Jackson would act like that. If anything, he's been seeking me out more than I've been pursuing him," I said.

"Listen. I hate to pull the Been There, Done That card. But this is your first real boyfriend. You have to take it slow and look out for yourself."

I watched Ava for a second as I ate a bite of my sub. Something seemed off about this whole conversation. Why had she tracked me down for lunch? Was she on a mission of some kind? "Why are you saying all this?" I asked her.

"I'm looking out for you, that's all." She shrugged.

"Are you sure you're not looking out for Lucy?" I asked.

"What?" Ava tossed her head, flipping her bangs away from her eyes.

"I feel like you're trying to push me away from Jackson. Did Lucy ask you to say something? I mean, I know she's not comfortable with—"

"No," Ava interrupted me. "Not at all. I mean, she is kind of upset about how this all happened, but no, she doesn't want him for herself. I promise, I just don't want you to get hurt."

"Of course you don't—sorry. I guess my emotions are running a little high right now," I said.

"No kidding. So are everyone else's. Especially Lucy. She even got a speeding ticket this morning because she was telling me how she felt about you and Jackson."

"What?" Lucy never got tickets—she never sped. "So, um, how *does* she feel?" I asked timidly. "I'm guessing not all that good, if it made her drive super fast."

Ava dabbed at her mouth with a napkin, brushing off a speck of guacamole. "She wants you to be happy. But she wishes it were with someone else. She can't help feeling sort of . . . I don't know how to put this without sounding all dramatic. But I guess she feels betrayed? He was kind of her worst enemy for a while there."

My stomach sort of lurched. My sandwich suddenly didn't

seem all that appealing. I knew that she'd freaked out about seeing Jackson when we got here, which was why I hadn't wanted to tell her I'd met him and that I liked him. But she'd had some time to get used to the idea, and they were working together . . . she had to be getting over it—and him—a little bit every day. If she couldn't, that was a big problem, for all of us.

"I wish she could forget about what happened. I wish . . . it hadn't happened like that," I said. "But from Jackson's point of view, it was typical middle school—lots of drama about not very much. I mean, we talked about it a little."

"That's because it wasn't traumatic for him. It was for her," Ava said.

"Back then, yeah, but . . . she has to forget about that. She has to move on," I said.

"Easier said than done." Ava's phone rang and she took it out, looked at the number, then slid it back into her pocket. "Listen, I can talk to each of you as much as you want, but you guys really need to talk it over with each other. So, to change the subject for a second, I have to ask you a favor. I already asked Lucy and she's cool with it."

I was intrigued now. "What?"

"If by any chance you could not tell anyone that I'm here just yet, that would be good," Ava said.

"Why?"

"I want to hide out for a few more days," she said. "My parents are going to be mad that I quit the internship, my roommate is going to be mad that I left town without paying the rest of the rent I owed for the summer, the magazine editor is going to yell at me, and I'd really rather not explain all this to anyone but you and Lucy right now."

"I thought you said your mom knew where you were. Is that true or not?"

"Not," Ava said.

"So does that mean you haven't even told them where you are yet?" I asked. "Is it because the law is going to come looking for you?"

"No," she said. "Nothing like that. I didn't commit a crime. I just screwed up royally, that's all. And the longer I can wait before I have to admit that to everyone, the better. I'll just get some days in at my new job, earn some money, get things back on track. *Then* I'll tell them."

"But they're going to know you're not in Chicago," I said. "What about the office phone?"

"Never gave it to them. Told them to use my cell. And from my cell, I could be anywhere. I turned off all the 'locate me' stuff on all my screens and apps and stuff. No one will find me."

I stared at her. This was a side to her I'd never seen before. "You're so devious. You're kind of scaring me right now."

"Anyone can be devious," she said. "It's easy to pick up how to do this kind of thing. I've watched a lot of TV shows where people disappeared."

"Me too," I said, laughing. "Remember that three-week period in February when I was recovering from mono and I couldn't leave the house much? I watched about two hundred episodes of *Law & Order*."

"Yeah, and we all sat around hoping we wouldn't get it because we all drank out of the same mocha?" Ava shuddered. "Mocha mono. Won't do that again."

"Hey, I was the one with mono, not *you*!" I reminded her. I glanced at a new text on my phone. Jackson had directed me to a photo he posted from work—and it featured Lucy holding a bumper sticker that said *I Brake for Apple Pie*.

"She looks fine," I said, showing Ava the photo. "She looks like she's having fun."

"She puts on a show sometimes. You know that about her. It's from when her parents broke up and didn't give her any advance notice. She had to pretend she was okay with that, and she did, up to a point. But she freaks out when people surprise her with things because it makes her think she can't trust anyone. And you most definitely surprised her."

I nodded. I hadn't thought about the fact that what I'd done might have reopened an old wound. I'd never meant for anything like that to happen.

CHAPTER 21

Lucy

Friday afternoon, I was helping a customer choose between a red shirt with a green apple on the front of it and a green shirt with a red apple on it, when I saw someone familiar out of the corner of my eye.

I didn't just see her, I said to myself. *That can't be. I didn't just see my mother walk in, did I?*

Seconds later, she skittered over to me in high-heeled sandals, black capri pants, and a smooth blue sleeveless blouse. She was totally coordinated, head to toe, as usual. Despite being confused by her arrival, I reached out and gave her a big hug, which felt good. "Lucyloo," she said, giving me a warm squeeze. "I've missed you so much."

"I didn't know you were coming," I said, cringing at her

using my nickname in front of other people. "Why didn't you call?"

"It was a last-minute decision early this morning. I was driving down Lyndale when it suddenly hit me," she said.

"What hit you? Another car?" My mom's driving record is not exactly blemish-free. She once rear-ended a city bus because she was on her phone making a real estate deal. Then again, who was I, recent speeding ticket–getter, to talk?

"Cute, very cute. No, an idea," she said. "A brilliant, exciting idea."

Just then Jackson walked out of the back room, carrying a crate of apples to restock the bins.

"And who are you?" Mom asked brightly. She's like that. She'll say hello and introduce herself to anyone, because "you never know who might need to buy or sell a house someday." Her whole life is a marketing opportunity.

It was no use telling her Jackson was seventeen and wouldn't be buying or selling real estate anytime soon. She'd call him a "growth and development market" or something like that.

"I'm Jackson Rolfsmeier," he said, a little unsure of himself. Maybe he didn't remember what she looked like.

"Wait a second. What? Not the Jackson Rolfsmeier who lived down the block. Oh my gosh, how are you? We haven't seen you in ages." She attempted to give Jackson a hug, but ended up just sort of holding both his arms in hers for a second. Jackson looked like he'd rather die than be kissed by her, so thankfully she got the message and didn't do her usual two smooches on the cheek. She likes to pretend she's French sometimes. It's annoying. She's Norwegian. No, scratch that—her great-grandparents were Norwegian. She's from a Twin Cities suburb.

"Mom, I told you he was working here," I said. Then I regretted it. Why would I be talking about Jackson to my mom? I hoped he wouldn't think that it was earth-shatteringly important that he was working here, even if it, you know, *was* in the beginning.

"You did?" she asked.

"Well, in passing," I said.

"That's amazing! Such good friends as you two used to be. What a cool coincidence," Mom said. She didn't even remember what I'd told her about Jackson.

"Well, it's not that big of a coincidence," Jackson said. "I mean, our grandparents know each other up here, so . . ."

"Set up by the grandparents to work together, huh?" Mom smiled. "Wouldn't be the first time my parents tried to pull off something like that. They had me work here one summer with a boy they thought I should be matched up with—"

"It's not like that," I interrupted her.

"At all," Jackson added with a little more firmness than I had.

"Just teasing," Mom said. "Although they did do that to *me*. So anyway, Luce, the answer was right in front of me the whole time. All the trials and tribulations we've been through, the double-booking at the club . . . All of that is completely irrelevant now," she went on. "Because you know what I realized last night when I was shopping online? I was buying a pair of sandals and on the sidebar was an ad all about escaping the ordinary and heading north to adventure—"

"It's a tourism slogan, Mom."

"But it's more than that. Don't you see? Gary and I need this escape wedding. We can do it—and we can have the wedding right here."

"*Here?*" asked Jackson.

"In Bridgeport, I mean. And it'll be perfect. My parents are here, you're here . . . and look at how beautiful it is."

I tried to smile. I really did. But no smile would appear. My mother was talking about moving her gigantic wedding to Bridgeport—and I would get swept up in the tide more than ever. What was I saying? I'd drown in the tide.

"Whose wedding?" Jackson's forehead creased in confusion. Of course: when we'd been friends, four years ago, my mom and dad were still together. He looked over at me and smirked suggestively.

"Wait a second," I said. "You don't think it's *my* wedding."

"Don't be silly," Mom said. "Lucy's not even dating anyone, Jackson. Unless things have changed?"

I just stared at the ceiling and rolled my eyes. Trust my mom to show up and embarrass me like this.

"I'm getting remarried this summer. I'm surprised Lucy hasn't told you about it yet."

"Oh, we don't have a lot of time to talk," I quickly said. "We're usually busy with customers." Not to mention not prone to sharing anything about our private lives. He had no idea my parents had divorced not long after he and I stopped hanging out.

"Funny. I don't see any customers," Mom said.

"That's because it's still early. They're coming." Jackson made a big show of looking at his watch. "Every day at about this time, we get slammed by bus tours." He nodded. "Slammed."

"We'll cross that bridge when we come to it," she said. "Oh—Luce. A bridge. In Bridgeport. We should get married on a bridge. So symbolic, so indicative of the future."

"Aren't you worried about traffic?" Jackson asked.

I put my hand over my mouth to keep from laughing.

The image of my mother in her perfect dress and her perfect veil getting blown around by a semi going past was impossible not to laugh at.

Even my mother had to smile. "Not that kind of bridge, no—one in a park, or maybe by the lake, something that goes from the lake to the shore."

"I think there's one at the Beach Club," said Jackson. "People use it for portraits, like senior pictures and stuff."

"Mom, I hope you don't mean you want to get married at the Bridgeport Beach Club," I said. "I'm sure they're booked solid."

"No, nothing so traditional as that. I have a few other ideas."

"Great," I said. "Can't wait to hear them." *And hear them and hear them and hear them.*

"Oh, I just knew you'd be on board with this. Well, I'm off to make some plans. I'll see you later!" She touched my shoulder, gave a little flounce, and headed out the door.

Jackson and I looked at each other. "Well. That was strange," he commented.

"For her? Clearly you remember my mother?" I asked.

"Not really," he said. "I mean, not like that. She made good cookies. That's about all I remember. Your house always had the best snacks. Plus you had a nice minivan." He laughed.

"Remember the time we went to the movies with about ten other people and we all fit into the van?"

"I think it was fifteen people and breaking the law," I said, laughing.

"So, uh, when did your parents get divorced?"

"About two years ago," I said. "Tons of fun."

"Yeah, I can imagine. My family's had some pretty bad times lately, too." He had a faraway look in his eyes. I wanted to ask him about it, but my mom barged back in, tote bag over her arm.

"Back already?" I asked.

"I forgot to ask where your charming little place is. Do you think I could go by and drop off some of my things or would that wake up Mikayla? She doesn't work the night shift, does she?"

"She's at a club, Mom, not a factory. What are you dropping off—stuff for the house, like we talked about?" I'd texted Mom a wish list of the things we needed.

"Oh, no. Just my luggage," she said, holding out her smartphone to me. "Punch in the address, would you?"

My finger hesitated above the screen. "Mom, why are you bringing your bags to the cabin? Why aren't you staying at Nana and Grandpa's? They have a lot more room."

"It's just for tonight," she said. "I want to make sure you

girls are squared away safely for the rest of the summer. Later!"

My mom had promised me I could be on my own this summer; it was one of the main reasons I'd come here—to become more independent and less involved in her daily drama. Now she'd followed me here? With *luggage*?

Great. My mom was moving to town. I suppose I shouldn't have been surprised. Nothing about this summer was going the way I'd planned.

CHAPTER 22

Mikayla

The second I got released from work, I raced outside and dived into the cold lake—even though no one else was around to go with me. I'd had such a long, hot day teaching tennis and doing a bike ride with the older kids. I felt like I could have scraped the dried salt off my skin.

I dived under the surface, feeling my hair fan out behind me, staying submerged long enough to truly cool down. Was it just me, or was the lake getting warmer as the summer went on? Or was I building up a tolerance, the way I did every winter to the frigid temperatures?

When I walked out of the lake, Jackson was standing on the beach. I couldn't have imagined a better sight at that moment. He had on a faded red T-shirt with long khaki shorts, and his face lit up as I got closer, his mouth widening into a smile. But at the same time something seemed a little restrained about him, like he had something on his mind he needed to share. We usually greeted each other with a big hug, but he didn't look like he wanted that right now.

"Hey. What are you doing here? I thought you had to be at work at five thirty." I picked up the towel I'd left by my shoes and wrapped it around my shoulders.

"I got someone to sub for me tonight," he said.

I rubbed my wet hair with the towel, feeling a little nervous about his subdued tone. "You're kidding—that's great! So instead of meeting at eleven, we can meet now? What should we do? You want to—"

But Jackson was shaking his head. "Nah, it's not what you think."

"It's not?" I pressed the towel against my face. I'd been looking forward to seeing him all day. In fact, I think I'd actually started looking forward to it the day before. This didn't sound good, for some reason. I started to think about Ava's warnings. Was this when he turned back into the Jackson that Lucy knew—and dumped me?

"I can't meet you tonight. Like, at all." Jackson scuffed at the sand with his shoe. He wasn't making much eye contact.

All of my warning signals were going off inside. My heart sank, like a rock in the lake. Down . . . down . . . nearing bottom.

"Why can't you?" I asked. I might have a problem initially talking to boys, but I had no problem sticking up for myself—no matter who I was talking to. I needed to learn why he was blowing off our plans.

"It's kind of a long story," he said.

"So . . . tell it to me," I urged. I wasn't about to settle for the "long story" story. That didn't tell me anything!

"You know how I'm living with my grandparents," Jackson said. "Well, my older brother is here, too. I need to hang out with him tonight."

Jackson hadn't talked much about his older brother. I wasn't sure how close they actually were. "Oh. Well, I could tag along," I suggested.

He shook his head. "No. I wouldn't want you to."

I didn't like the sound of that. "Why not?" I asked. "I have brothers. It's not like I don't know—"

"You *don't* know," Jackson said coldly. Then he touched my arm. "Sorry—I'm sorry."

"Do you not want him to meet me?" I asked. "That's pretty insulting."

"No—I didn't mean that. This is coming out all wrong."

Jackson ran his hands through his hair. "I'm just stressed out. He makes me so frustrated and I didn't mean to take it out on you. Sorry." He reached for my hands. "He's just . . . He can't be alone right now. Listen, I promise I'll see you tomorrow. And I'll call you later. And I'll make it up to you next week, when we go to the carnival, watch fireworks . . ."

"That all sounds great," I said, squeezing his hand. Whatever was going on with his brother, it didn't sound good. "I didn't know there was a carnival in town. You like rides, don't you?"

"You don't know the half of it," Jackson said. "I once won a new bike by staying on a roller coaster longer than anyone else—"

"How long?"

"Thirteen and a half hours," Jackson said.

"Wow." I stood back in admiration. "I don't know if I *have* that much time."

Jackson laughed. "You know what? Ten minutes ago I was miserable. You know how to get me to loosen up."

"Anytime," I said. "Just promise you'll get me a cotton candy. And a funnel cake."

"You're too sweet." Jackson ran his fingers through my hair. "No. For real." He put his hands on my shoulders, like he was telling me something serious. "Your sweet tooth is out of control."

"What? It is not," I said, pushing against his chest with the palm of my hand.

"How about that blueberry pie at the diner? You had your piece and mine," Jackson said. "And then there's the Midge's Ice Cream incident. You single-handedly ate a banana split."

"I went for a really long run that morning," I said. "Ten miles!"

"I'm just saying. You have a bit of a sweet tooth."

I narrowed my eyes at him. "Is this going to be a problem?"

"No, it's no problem." He pulled me toward him. "Nothing you do is a problem. Well. Except maybe the fact you haven't invited me over yet. You do have your own place."

"Not exactly," I said. I smiled nervously. Yeah, *that* wasn't going to happen for quite some time.

When I got back to the cabin half an hour later, Lucy was sitting at the kitchen counter. We quickly said hi, and then I started to head for my room. Then I stopped. This was it. My chance to really talk with her. Ava was at work, so we had the house to ourselves. *Then again*, I thought, *maybe we ought to go for a walk—neutral territory and all.* We could get everything out in the open. "Lucy?" I asked. "Do you maybe—"

"You need a new soap dispenser." Lucy's mom rounded

the corner from the hallway into the living room. "Mikayla!" she cried. "How are you? You don't mind a new roommate, do you?"

"M—Mrs. Carpenter?" I said. "It's nice to see you. I didn't know you were coming," I said, turning to Lucy. But she didn't make eye contact. Normally she'd have texted me about this eighty-five times by now, asking for help and advice. But I hadn't heard a word from her all day. Was she giving me the silent treatment, or what?

"I've been really busy," she said, leafing through one of the magazines. "Slipped my mind."

"Oh, Lucy. Be honest. Mikayla, *she* didn't even know I was coming until today. It was an impulse decision," Mrs. Carpenter said, sitting down at the kitchen table. "So thanks for letting me stay here."

"You're staying here?" I repeated.

"Don't worry. Boy, the panic in your eyes! It's just for a night." She winked at me. "I know you're a bit crowded in here, and you need your space. So how's your summer going?"

"Um, fine," I said.

"This little house has a certain cozy charm, doesn't it?" she commented.

I looked at Lucy and tried not to laugh, remembering her saying that's just how her mom would describe it. I thought I saw a hint of a smile in the corner of her mouth, but she just kept flipping through the magazine on the counter. "I love the deck. I thought we could grill out tonight."

"Mom, we don't have a grill," said Lucy.

"Oh. Well, maybe we'll get takeout, then. You'll have to excuse us, Mikayla, but we have a lot of planning to do." Mrs. Carpenter flipped through an issue of *Midwest Bride* magazine. "I thought this one would have some good ideas for outdoor receptions. What do you think of this trellis?"

"Wedding stuff? I can help," I said. "Hand me some of those magazines."

Lucy begrudgingly slid a stack of three fat bridal magazines toward me. "Dig in," she said.

This wasn't a bad way to spend the night—at all. A couple of weeks ago I would have been completely happy to hang out with Lucy and her mom, looking at magazines.

But now, sitting here and thinking about Jackson, I felt like I couldn't concentrate. I wanted to be with him instead.

I slipped my phone out and sent him a short text, hoping everything was going okay.

He wrote back seconds later and my phone dinged with an alert: *Should have asked you to come. Miss u.*

We exchanged a few more messages, making plans for the next day.

Can we meet later tonight? he wrote.

Somehow I didn't think that would go over well, me sneaking out later to meet Jackson. Especially not with Lucy's mom staying here. When I looked up from responding, Lucy was frowning at me. "That alert is really annoying. Can you turn it off, or not text for two seconds?"

"Sure. Of course." I thought about what Ava had told me earlier. For whatever reason, and maybe there was more than one, this was really difficult for Lucy to accept. I needed to make sure I wasn't making it harder.

At the same time, I didn't want to ignore Jackson when he was having a hard time.

I decided to divide the night in two parts. Right now, I was focusing on Lucy and on not making her even more annoyed with me. I could talk to him later, when I was alone in my room. I slid my phone into my knapsack and zipped the pocket closed.

"So. What kind of stuff are we looking for?" I asked Lucy's mom.

CHAPTER 23

Lucy

I met Mom at Blue Cove Catering on Monday. The place was on the first floor of a large old house halfway out of town, on the lake. I didn't see a cove, but people tend to use those descriptions loosely in order to bring in more business. Just like there had never been a blackbird at the Blackbird Café, or the Mafia at Walleye Mafia—at least, not as far as I knew.

We were there to sample food from their menu for her upcoming wedding in Bridgeport—which I hadn't been able to talk her out of yet, despite trying and trying and trying over the weekend, but I didn't mind checking out the food options. It was lunchtime and I was starving.

But who was I kidding? The real reason I wanted to go,

the real reason I'd even brought up Blue Cove with her, was Gus. Ever since we'd exchanged phone info the other day—okay, let's call it what it was: our phones kissed—and he'd hung around the store for way too long, I'd felt myself thinking about him more and more. He was so easygoing. And funny. And considerate. And he had these cheekbones that were model-like, and his eyes . . .

I'd been so busy focusing on Jackson and Mikayla that I'd neglected my own life for the past week, not seeing Claire, or going out much with anyone at all, and just mostly moping around at home. I was ready to be done with that. I didn't know how, exactly, I was supposed to move on. But I was starting to realize that was what I needed to do.

So instead of dropping by his work on my own, I'd had my mother call and arrange an appointment. Slightly chicken of me. I realize that. But if Mom wanted my help, I needed her help just as much.

I kind of thought that Gus liked me, too, but I wasn't going to get carried away and kiss him or anything, without having a whole lot of proof that it wouldn't end in disaster.

Mom was waiting for me in the parking lot—she was on the phone, of course. She'd spent the morning racing around Bridgeport like her wedding was tomorrow and she had hair, dress, food, and venue emergencies. (Well, according to her, she actually *did*.) After she wrapped up her latest conversation, we headed up the steps and rang the bell.

Gus answered the door with a smile. I felt myself blush a little as he looked at me. "Hi! Come on in."

"Mom, this is Gus," I said. "Gus, this is my mom."

"Call me Kerri," she said, shaking his hand. "What a gorgeous space you have here."

I'd have to tell Gus later that my mom couldn't look at a house as anything other than an investment. We followed him into the back of the house—a gigantic kitchen with gleaming stainless steel appliances, white accessories, and French country décor (sue me, I know these things thanks to my mom). There was a long island with a black marble counter and three white stools lined up at it. "Have a seat," Gus said. "Chef Michael? Kerri and Lucy Carpenter are here."

"Who?" He glanced over his shoulder at us. "Ah yes. Hello. Bring me the samples, Gus." He clapped his hands together briskly.

"This is great!" my mother said cheerfully. "I actually like to see how people work, where they do the cooking."

"Good, because you'll need to. I'm in a rush," the chef replied.

"I'm sorry?" Mom asked. "I thought we had booked an appointment with you."

"You may have, but I took on a last-minute engagement party. You know how that goes. Suddenly the mother of the bride realizes she's not up to serving fifty people, she calls me," the chef complained, sounding proud at the same time.

"Yes, but . . . a person can say no," my mother said, "when that person has a prior engagement."

He didn't seem to hear her, which was probably a good thing. "I have all your samples ready to taste. I took the liberty of selecting some wine samples as well." Chef Michael had shoulder-length hair, was a bit on the heavy side, and wore a white apron over a ratty gray T-shirt, baggy shorts, and leather Greek-style sandals. He looked kind of sloppy, but then again, he was in his kitchen.

"Some people are front of the house," my mother said under her breath, "and some people are back of the house. Or they should be."

I was beginning to think that Blue Cove didn't stand a chance of becoming the caterer for my mom's wedding. But then he started handing us plate after plate of sample appetizers. I tried a chicken satay stick, a spring roll, a shrimp puff . . . I was so hungry. Everything looked so good.

"What's this?" I asked, pointing to a spread on a cracker.

"Walleye caviar," the chef said. "It's my special recipe. Try it."

I investigated the cracker more closely. It looked terrible to me, but I knew I should be more adventurous when it came to gourmet food. *Do the opposite of what you'd normally do, for once*, I thought. *Take a chance.*

I took a small bite. It tasted salty, but that was about it.

"People would kill to have a free sample like that, right?" Chef Michael asked me.

"Mmmmmaybe," I murmured, feeling like caviar was just another word for glue or paste. My lips felt stuck together.

"I read about that in *St. Paul* magazine," said my mom. "That's one of the reasons I'm here. What's in it?"

"A chef never tells. Unless he is paid to tell." He smiled a sort of smarmy smile that made me wonder if he really thought he was being charming. Because he wasn't. "Gus!" he suddenly yelled, again with the hand-clapping. "Cheese plate. What are you waiting for?"

"Here you are." Gus set down a basket of sliced baguette bread and a plate that was covered with small wedges of a variety of cheeses. I admired him for being so polite when his boss was screaming at him.

"No. This bread is sliced too thickly. Do you want the old ladies to break their dentures?" He grabbed a fresh baguette from a different basket and whacked it onto the counter in front of Gus. Was it my imagination or did he nearly hit Gus on the nose? "Do it again," he said.

It was like catering boot camp.

"Old ladies?" my mother said. "To whom are you referring?"

"The engagement party. Any engagement party. There's always a lot of old birds," Chef Michael said.

"They're called matures," my mother replied, "in the real estate business. You should show some respect. Your customers will notice. Now, I'd like to try a couple of your salads. The watercress, in particular."

My mother verified that the Caesar salad was made with real Caesar dressing—lemon, egg, and anchovy—and then told me to taste a few bites, as if I knew what a top-of-the-line Caesar salad should taste like. "Mom, why am I sampling everything and you're not?" I asked.

"I'm waiting for the desserts," she said. "Everyone remembers the desserts."

"Well, I need a break." While they talked salad options and prices, I went over to the prep counter where Gus was working. "Wow," I said as I watched him chop almonds. "You really know what you're doing."

Gus looked slightly insulted as he glanced up at me. "Of course I do."

"Sorry! I just—I have no skills when it comes to chopping

and slicing. You look like someone on *Top Chef*."

"I wouldn't go *that* far," Gus said, laughing.

"Neither would I," Chef Michael commented, peering over at the cutting board. "You missed a few." He pointed to some larger pieces of almond.

Gus cleared his throat. "I always do that," he said, sounding a little irritated, as if he'd explained this before. "Then people know they're hand-chopped," Gus said. "It's more authentic."

"If someone wants authentic, they can cook at home," Chef Michael said. "They're coming to us for a professional product. When they order the almond crème brûlée tart, they want small pieces." He leaned over, took the knife from Gus, and rapidly chopped the remaining almonds.

Gus looked at me and mouthed "Why am I here?", partially crossing his eyes.

I was in the middle of sampling a mini cheese quiche and nearly choked from laughing.

"Now, on to the dessert tray," Chef Michael said.

"*Now?*" I said. "After all that?"

"Take littler bites in the future," the chef said.

"Could have told me that before," I whispered to Gus. My mom was barely sampling anything—while I had eaten about three meals' worth. "Mom, *you* taste the cake. I'm done."

"I have four cake samples for you. One's very traditional. . . ." Chef Michael started pulling plasticware out of the giant stainless refrigerator. He cut small pieces from each and set them in front of her. While she was tasting the cakes, I edged closer to Gus. "Is this guy for real?" I whispered.

"Unfortunately, yes. You okay?" he asked. "You look a little full."

"Oh, yeah. It's like Thanksgiving. In June. But whatever," I said. Then I whispered, "How can you stand him? He's horrible."

Gus nodded. "Told you," he said, barely opening his mouth.

"Lucy, you *have* to try this," my mom insisted, handing me a small plate. "Chocolate mousse cake."

"People think it's cute up north to call it 'moose' on their menus. Like the four-legged creature." Chef Michael sniffed. "I, however, do not."

"Well, la-di-da," I whispered, thinking that if Chef Michael looked like anything else in the mammal world, it was most definitely a moose. A conceited, badly dressed moose. "Please don't pick him, Mom," I said when he left the room to fetch some wine samples for her. "I mean, no offense to you," I said to Gus. "You're awesome."

He blushed bright red, and as I noticed that, I felt my

own cheeks flush with color.

"Uh, it's . . . no problem," he said, his voice all rough and strained as if he had suddenly developed laryngitis. "So I was wondering. Do you want to go kayaking sometime?"

"Kayaking? Um . . ."

"I know what I'm doing. I mean, if you don't. And I'm not saying you don't, I have no idea, but if you were worried or anything—"

"I've kayaked before," I told him.

"So you want to go, then?" he pressed.

I started to say "Sure," but then I chickened out halfway through and switched it to "Maybe," so it came out "Schmaybe."

Schmaybe. That would be my superhero name. Captain Schmaybe.

Sometimes I really hate myself.

"What was that?" Gus asked. "Was that Norwegian?"

"No." I focused on the little teeny freckles on his nose. "I mean, yes," I said. "I would like that."

"Being Norwegian?" Gus said.

"Kayaking." Then I smiled the most awkward smile of my life, just to stop myself from saying something else. Kayaking was not exactly a romantic situation. I'd be fine. I'd be able to spend more time with Gus, getting to know him, without it being an actual date where I'd have to find out if he liked me. Or not.

The only problem was that suddenly I started feeling not so good. My stomach felt as if it was hosting a wrestling tournament. Chocolate mousse on one side, walleye caviar on the other. I never ate so much rich—and strange—food at one time. I'd been trying to impress Gus by sampling everything, so he'd think I was a foodie. Instead I was feeling more like a deadie, or at the very least extremely nauseous.

"Excuse me," I said to Gus. "Uh, Mom." I edged closer to her. "We have to get going."

"We do?" she asked, but she didn't look disappointed. She'd already crossed Chef Michael off her list, I could tell. "All right then, we do." She exchanged some pleasantries with the chef and with Gus while I headed for the car. I needed to get home, and fast.

CHAPTER 24

Mikayla

I ordered a cold press coffee at Earl Grey's and, as I waited for it, spotted a near-empty tray of snickerdoodle cookies in the baked goods case.

I had to get one, right?

I thought of the first time Jackson and I had stood so close to each other here, and how we'd talked as if it was no big deal. It felt like a long time ago. I still couldn't understand how it was possible to physically miss someone so much. When we weren't together, it was hard not to count the minutes until we were going to be.

It was a feeling I wished I could share with Lucy, but she hadn't talked to me much lately. I'd tried a few times to have a conversation, but she brushed me off, saying she was late for something or other.

I sat down at the small round table where Ava and Lucy had staked out a spot. I didn't know what Ava was up to, but she'd demanded we both be here for a mandatory house meeting. She'd promised that it was about something fun.

Lately, whenever Lucy and I were in the same room, it wasn't fun.

"The reason I've called you all here," Ava began, as if she were giving a formal speech, "is because it's time to have that party we keep talking about. Now, we know that the Fourth of July is tomorrow and we missed that boat, but that doesn't mean we can't plan something for next weekend. It's high time we got going on this, because we don't want to have just *one* blowout party, right? This is going to be the first of many. Or at least, a couple. So what are your ideas?"

I noticed Lucy was only drinking a cup of water. "How are you feeling, by the way?" I asked. She'd had a case of food poisoning and stayed with her grandparents the past twenty-four hours so they and her mom could take care of her and make sure she was recovering okay.

"A little shaky," Lucy said. "But getting back to normal."

"Good, I'm glad," I said. "It's so awful what happened."

"Okay, okay, it is awful, and we're sorry," Ava interrupted, "but let's talk about something more *fun*. Who would like to present an idea for our first party? Okay, fine, I'll start. What do you guys think of a Hawaiian luau theme?"

Lucy and I both looked at Ava with raised eyebrows. "No," we said in unison.

Well, at least we could still agree on something.

"Too tacky," I said, breaking off a part of the cookie and offering it to Lucy and Ava.

Lucy shook her head. "It's too cutesy," she said.

Ava gestured to me. "Fine. Your turn, then."

I thought about it as a bite of snickerdoodle cookie dissolved on my tongue. "How about if we have just an old-fashioned, no-frills barbecue and cookout?" I suggested.

"Cooking for everyone? That's way too much work," said Lucy. "We don't have a grill, anyway."

"We could probably borrow one," I said. "Maybe from your grandparents?"

"I don't know. Who wants to cook all night?" said Lucy.

"Fine. No barbecue," I said. "Let's hear your idea."

Lucy looked up at the ceiling for a minute. "This is hard. How about a This Is Not a Fourth of July party? Or wait, how about we call it the Independence Party? Maybe it wouldn't be the Fourth of July, but we are living on our own . . . and that is kind of why we're celebrating."

"True. But I'm worried no one will get it. They'll think

it's a political event," I said.

"Seriously? Who is going to think that, really?" Lucy said with a laugh.

"Never mind what *they'd* think. It's not a good theme if you have to explain it," Ava said. "All right, my turn. The theme could be . . . hey, we could call it a housewarming party! Because lately? The house has lacked warmth. I'm just saying."

I shifted in my chair. I knew what she was getting at: this seemingly endless feud between me and Lucy. I felt bad, but I didn't know what to do about it. Lucy was being so stubborn and unwilling to accept the fact I was seeing Jackson. She was freezing me out of her life. I was waiting for it to pass, like an awkward stage, but it didn't seem to be going anywhere. It was like her feet were buried in the sand—deep, deep down. She wasn't budging. She thought I was wrong and that was that.

Although I hadn't been completely honest with her when I told her I knew Jackson, I'd told her right away when we turned from acquaintances into something more. I'd apologized for it being awkward, and for the fact I'd ended up with him. If she'd let me talk to her longer than fifteen seconds, maybe I could explain things better.

"We don't have to have a theme or make it anything super

special," I said. "Can't we just have appetizers and drinks and play some music, maybe get some yard games? Beanbag toss, croquet, horseshoes . . ."

"I don't know. Isn't that sort of childish?" Lucy asked.

Why did I feel like she'd find a reason to dislike every suggestion I made? "People don't stop liking games just because they're not little kids anymore."

"I know, but we don't need activities," Lucy said.

"We need some reason for people to hang around, having a good time," I said. She was usually the queen of playing games. We'd spent hours playing video games—even Scrabble, Yahtzee, cards. Not to mention sports like Wiffle ball and kickball.

"All right, all right already," Ava said. "Could you guys agree on just one thing tonight? Maybe? I was thinking we could have it on Saturday night, the thirteenth. Does that work for you guys?"

"Yeah." Lucy nodded. "That should work."

"Oh . . . really?" I asked. "So soon? That's great!"

"Cool! Hey, you guys agreed! It's a Christmas miracle," Ava joked. We both stared at her. "Okay, it's a Fourth of July miracle. So can we start inviting people—like, tonight?" asked Ava excitedly. "There's this singer-guitarist who plays at the café . . . plus all my coworkers . . . well, almost all. What about you? Who are you guys going to invite first?" she asked.

"Claire," Lucy said.

"Jackson," I said.

Bzzzt. That was the exact wrong answer to give, and I realized it as soon as it came out of my mouth. "And a bunch of friends from the beach club. Tons, actually," I added quickly.

"Hey, so . . . now that we have that settled, the carnival's opening tonight!" Ava said. "You guys want to go check it out?"

"I would love to," I said.

"No, thanks," Lucy said. "You guys go ahead."

"Well . . . what would *you* like to do?" I asked her. "We could go to the movies, we could go back to the mini golf place, take a drive—"

"No, thanks. I have other plans," she said.

"With Gus? I knew it!" I said excitedly. "You know, just because we're in a fight doesn't mean that I can't tell when you like someone."

"No. Plans with my *mom*," Lucy said, irritated. "We're not all dating someone, okay?"

"Guys, please. You're friends. Stop fighting, seriously." Ava pushed back her chair and stood up. "If I wanted this much drama, I could have gone to dramatic performance camp for the summer."

"Sorry," Lucy said, without looking at me. "I'm still not feeling all that well. I apologize if I'm a little bit grumpy."

"Sorry, Ava. And I didn't mean to imply . . . anything, Luce," I said. "Sorry you're not feeling great."

"Now. Was that so impossible?" Ava asked with a wave of her hand.

Impossible? No. But did it change anything?

I glanced nervously at Lucy. She looked at me and sort of smiled. It wasn't the same wattage as a normal Lucy smile. She was only giving me a half smile.

I'd kept telling myself that we would get through this, that all she needed was a little time to get used to the idea of me and Jackson together. But time was passing every day. She didn't seem to feel okay about it. I didn't know what I should do—or even what I could do, if she kept me at arm's length the way she had been.

CHAPTER 25

Lucy

On the big day of the Fourth of July Apple Daze sidewalk sale celebration, my grandparents were manning the store while Jackson and I worked outside. We had a large cart with various snacks, sale items, gifts, souvenirs, collectible items, and a five-gallon container of apple cider. I hadn't been able to help get things ready because I'd missed work the past two days.

Cars were stacked up along the street looking for parking places, and the sidewalks were crawling with people, even at ten in the morning. Down the street, I could see lots of activity at the kite store, the bakery, and the sandal shop. No one was headed our way just yet.

"I can't believe you had to go to the emergency room

Monday night. At least your mom's in town to take care of you."

"Yeah, I guess that's the silver lining in the whole food poisoning fiasco," I said, silently cursing Chef Michael and his practically lethal appetizers. "A mom who usually hovers too much, but is great in a crisis when you actually need hovering. So what are we supposed to do with this cart?"

"Beats me," Jackson said. "Stand here and wait for customers. Look healthy. An apple a day keeps the doctor away—stuff like that."

"Let's not talk about doctors," I said, smiling ruefully. "How about you smile and hand out apple samples? I'll push the souvenirs, because everyone needs an Apple Capital of America bumper sticker."

"I apple," Jackson said. "Do you?"

"Not much, no," I said.

We started to get some foot traffic about fifteen minutes later. People would wander past, take a sample, check out the cart. We sold a few things, but I had a feeling the big rush wouldn't start until after everyone had breakfast and/or coffee.

Jackson went into the store to get us more bags, and a minute later Gus walked up carrying a wicker basket—sort of like a picnic basket—filled with crackers, cookies, pretzels, chocolates, peaches, and grapes. He set it on the table in front of me. "A thousand apologies for the horrible time you had trying out our food. I can't even—I mean, I can't believe you didn't even *tell* me, but your mom came by and chewed us out about your food poisoning. I feel terrible, so . . . if you're up for eating, like, ever again, here you go."

"Yeah, thanks." I eyed the basket. "If it's okay with you, I'm not sure I want to eat anything that comes from Blue Cove Catering."

"Neither do I. And it's not from there, it's from the natural foods co-op." He pulled a few grapes off the stems and dropped them into his smiling mouth. "See? Totally safe."

"What's so funny?" I asked. "I nearly died."

"No, it's not funny. I came by to tell you that I don't actually work there anymore," Gus said. "And I'm sorry you were so sick. Did you get all my messages?" I nodded. "Honestly, I had nothing to do with that. I am one hundred percent vigilant about food safety."

"You don't work there anymore?" I asked as I sorted through the basket.

"No. I quit last night. The guy is a bully. *And*, even worse, he almost killed you," Gus said. "So, no, I didn't want to keep working for him."

I laughed too, despite the fact he'd lost his job and I'd

been horribly ill. The whole situation seemed so ridiculous all of a sudden. "But what are you going to do now?" I asked him.

"I don't know." He looked around for a minute, nodded hello to my grandfather when he stepped outside to check out the crowds. "Should I see if he's hiring?"

"I wish he was," I said. "It'd be so awesome if you worked here." I smiled at him and felt this crazy happy glow, which sounds more bizarre than it felt.

"I know, right?" Gus replied. "I could totally sell this." He held up an apple-shaped pot holder and said in a cheesy voice, "Not only does it keep your hands safe, it's also good for baseball."

"So what was the last straw?"

"A ridiculous tower of whipped cream and strawberries and blueberries on top of a ridiculous cake. I told him it wouldn't work. I told him. The whole thing collapsed as I was bringing it into the party, like the air let out of a tire or something—so then he yelled at me in front of everyone." He laughed. "Just thinking about all that whipped cream cascading onto the floor—it's pretty funny, actually. Looked like melting snow."

"What did you do?" I asked.

"I handed him the cake platter and walked out," Gus said.

"I need another job. Right now I'm choosing between cleaning hotel rooms, selling kayaks, and making balloon animals."

"You know how to make balloon animals?" I asked, impressed.

"No. But I saw a girl outside the kite store doing it, and she was getting like a dollar a balloon, so . . ."

I laughed. "So you're going to teach yourself how to make giraffes and dogs out of balloons? *That's* your plan?"

Jackson returned carrying a stack of red paper bags. He and Gus said hello, and then Gus stepped to the side to make way for some customers filing up to the cart.

"I should probably get out of the way here," he said.

"Or just start buying things," I said. "You could be our most popular customer if you shell out some of your hard-earned cash."

"Sure. If the good old chef actually paid me when he was supposed to," Gus said. "I have a little bit saved for the carnival tonight. Are you guys planning to go? Seems like everyone's going."

I waited for Jackson to answer, but he was busy giving directions to someone.

"I'm pretty sure I will," I said. "So, um, I'll see you there?" I asked.

"Do you know what time?" he said.

"Oh, I don't know. Eight? Nine?" I guessed.

"Right. Okay." Gus nodded. "Sounds good. See you guys later."

After he walked away, Jackson flicked my arm. It was funny; once he did it, I remembered that he always used to do that to me. "He was asking you out. If you care."

"No, he wasn't," I said. "He asked both of us."

"He could give a rip about me," Jackson said.

"What's a rip?"

Jackson flicked my elbow. "Don't change the subject."

Fortunately for me, a slew of customers wanted to pay for things just then, so I didn't have to change the subject—they did it for me. But as I ran their credit cards through the store's iPhone, I did have time to wonder whether Gus had been asking me to go with him, just us, as a date. I'd have said yes, if I'd known.

I thought about what Mikayla had said the night before: "Just because we're in a fight doesn't mean that I can't tell when you like someone."

She was right; I did like Gus. It would have been really nice if I could have talked to her about it, about my feelings, and about how I should act or what I should do next.

Why could I talk to Jackson now, and not to her? Everything felt like it was the opposite of what it should be.

◆◆◆

Ava and I headed to the carnival together at about eight that night. She knew that I wasn't a big fan of rides—not since the Minnesota State Fair incident when I threw up ten seconds after I got off the vertical plunge—so we headed to the games. Halfway there, Ava stopped outside a fortune-teller's tent. "I have to go in there," she said.

"No. You don't have to," I said. "Save your money."

"Come on—we'll get a good rate if we both go in," Ava said. "You can find out about your love life and I'll find out whether anyone at home knows I'm here yet."

"Is that really the question you'd ask?"

"Well, it's one of them. The rest would be more interesting," Ava said. "Come on, come with me."

"How about I wait for you out here?" I said. "I get kind of creeped out because sometimes they say things that are sort of true. I don't feel like visiting the dark side right now."

"You're no fun. How will you know what fate has in store for you?"

"Um . . . *you'll* tell me?" I said.

"Don't be ridiculous." Ava grabbed my arm, and with her other hand swept aside the tent door.

Inside, a woman with long black hair streaked with gray was sitting at a small table. She wore a purple-and-gold scarf that was slightly like the colors of the new Minnesota Vikings uniforms. *Jolene, the Viking Psychic*, it said in swoopy handwriting on a sign on the table. "How may I help you girls?" she asked.

"You go first," said Ava, gesturing toward the chair at the table. "Here." She handed the psychic the required five dollars, and I sat down opposite her, feeling nervous.

"Your name?" she asked.

"Lucy," she said.

"Ah. Lucy. I am Jolene. Give me your hand."

I held out my hand and glanced over at Ava beside me with a worried look. I wasn't sure I wanted this Jolene person to hold my hand. She examined my right hand closely, then turned it over and studied my palm. "You are a hard worker," she said. "You don't give up easily." She looked up and focused on my face. Her gaze was so intense, I wanted to look away. Even for what seemed like a kind of ridiculous carnival act, there was something about her that truly did seem . . . clairvoyant. Or something. "What questions do you have for me?" she asked.

"Uh, well, I was wondering about . . . uh . . ." What did I want to know most? About my future, my family, my love life?

"Yes, there is a boy," she said, without even waiting for me to say it. She closed her eyes. "There are two boys. One will come to your rescue soon. Very soon. He will surprise you. The other one will . . ." She stopped and suddenly opened her eyes. "You do not want to know."

"What does that mean?" I asked. "Is it bad?"

"It must remain a mystery," she said. "Now, about your family . . ."

"That's okay," I said, getting to my feet. "I think I'm freaked out enough."

"Lucy, stay," Ava urged. "Don't you see? She's using a bunch of vague predictions," she whispered. "They don't mean anything. There aren't any details!"

"Then why did you want to come?" I asked.

"Because it's fun. I love the dark arts," she said.

"This isn't Harry Potter. This is the Viking Psychic," I said.

"Exactly. So don't worry about anything she said." Ava shrugged.

"Are you sure you are done? I can tell you about your future," Jolene said. "I have seen things, many things. . . . Do you wish to know where you will move next?"

"M-move?" I asked, edging toward the doorway.

"She means college," Ava said. "Don't you?"

Jolene made a bunch of swirling motions with her hands.

"I see a building. Ivy climbs up a brick wall. . . ."

"You're going Ivy League, baby!" Ava whispered, squeezing my shoulder.

"No, I'm *going* to wait for you outside." I swept aside the curtain and walked out to the carnival midway. Psychic or not, Jolene was one strange woman—or bad actress. I couldn't believe Ava wanted to hear what she had to say, but then, Ava has more of an adventurous streak than I do. I could almost imagine her grilling Jolene for specific details; she definitely wouldn't shy away from any predictions, the way I did.

One boy would surprise me . . . and one would remain a mystery.

I wasn't good at riddles. Was this one? Or was it just nonsense?

While I waited, I wandered around, looking at the so-called games of skill. Half a dozen carnival workers called to me, trying to get me to take a chance on their games. I was just about to hand over a five-dollar bill to knock down some milk bottles and win something goofy and embarrassing for Ava—I had a pretty good arm, and now that I'd been tossing apples around every day, my aim was getting even better—when Gus walked up to me, trailed by a group of friends.

"Hey! We're going to do the bungee jump. You want to come with?" he asked.

"They don't have a bungee jump, do they?" I asked.

"Well, if they do, we're finding it. Come on," Gus urged.

I shook my head. "No, thanks. Bungee jump? No. I can't imagine anything worse."

"Okay. How about the Spin and Drop?" Gus asked.

"Catch you later, Gus!" his friends called, and walked off toward the tall ride that looked suspiciously like the vertical plunge—only not nearly as tall, or sturdy.

"Or how about the tilt-a-whirl? Dizzy Dinos?" Gus kept naming rides as we wandered around the carnival that had taken over the giant parking lots by the high school. I heard a loud shriek that sounded very familiar and looked up—Mikayla and Jackson were sitting next to each other, getting tossed up and down, all while speeding forward in a circle.

"The Thresher!" Gus said. "I always liked that one."

"I hate rides," I said. "Pretty much." Especially that one. Especially right that minute.

"Oh." Gus looked a bit stunned. "Really? Well, I don't care. Stupid rickety rides would probably get stuck anyway."

"Great—*that's* reassuring."

"Okay then, plan B." Gus and I paused beside one of the food concessions, a place called Fresh-Fried. "Let's get cheese curds and then we can try to win some giant stuffed animal you'll hate immediately."

"Cheese curds? Chef Michael would not approve."

"Maybe not. He'd probably call it 'typical Midwestern bland,'" Gus said, making air quotes. "But that's a good thing. Unless you want mini donuts instead?"

"If it's fried, I'm up for it."

"Then let's split a funnel cake. *No* whipped cream. I have bad luck with that." He turned to me and smiled, and we were having a kind of weird, intense eye contact when my phone chimed. I tried to ignore it and focus on Gus, but it chimed again.

"Sorry, I—I have to get that."

I glanced down at the screen. *Where are you?* Ava wrote. *My fortune didn't say you would desert me!*

"Oh, no," I said, looking at Gus. *On my way*, I texted. *Where are you right now?* "I forgot Ava," I said.

"Forgot her?" Gus asked.

"I was supposed to be waiting for her outside the tent when I saw you. She completely panicked." I was making it sound like a matter of life and death—which it wasn't—but I needed an out right then. "I'll have to catch up with you later."

"Ava—panicked? Really? But—"

I know, I wanted to say. *It's completely not believable that she'd panic.* Gus and I were kind of having a moment, and I was blowing it. I should probably have told Ava that I needed to hang out with Gus for a while—she wouldn't mind at all—and just see where this might go. But instead, I headed off in search of Ava—and safety.

Why couldn't I stick around and see what happened with Gus? Why couldn't I just take a chance, for once in my life?

Because. Look what happened the last time you did that. Besides, slightly psychic Jolene had told me that something bad would happen with a boy, something that I would not want to know.

I had a feeling I *did* know. Right now, Gus and I got along; if I kissed him, I might ruin all that, which in turn might ruin my summer in Bridgeport. *But wait a second*, I thought. It wasn't going all that great, anyway.

I'd watch the fireworks with Ava, Claire, and other friends, like I'd promised. I'd stick to safety in numbers—for now, anyway.

CHAPTER 26

Mikayla

I leaned back against Jackson and looked up at the dark night sky. Red stars drifted down as bright white circles fell and zooming blue bursts lit up the sky. It was ten fifteen and the carnival was winding down for the night with a spectacular fireworks show.

Jackson had one arm around my waist and the other on my leg. His chin was resting on my head. If anyone had told me this was how I'd spend the Fourth of July this summer, I'd never have believed them.

"Heads up," Jackson said into my ear, suddenly moving around a bit. I scooted forward and he pulled his phone out of the back pocket of his jeans. He missed the call, but covered one ear with his hand while he listened to the message. He started cursing while he listened.

"I've got to go," he told me, getting to his feet.

"What's going on?" I asked, standing beside him.

"That was the police. My brother—Franklin—he's been in an accident. He's on his way to the hospital. I have to go." Jackson started heading to the parking lot, walking, and then jogging.

"Is he okay?" I asked, hurrying to catch up to him.

"Sounds like he is, but I need to get there and see for myself."

"Let me come with you. I'll drive," I said.

"No, I can—"

"No, you're too upset, plus you probably need to make some calls." I held out my hands for the keys to his Jetta.

I drove, getting directions from Jackson, who made a quick call to his grandfather, letting him know we were on the way and getting more details now that it was quiet enough to hear. "You won't believe this," he said to me, clicking off his phone. "He tried to get on the last ferry to the island for some reason. Problem was, it had already left the dock."

"What are you saying?" I said. "He drove a car into the lake?"

"Apparently, yeah. My grandpa's car," Jackson said. "A big, giant, heavy sedan."

"But he's . . . He got out of the car okay? Wow. That's lucky," I said.

"He makes dumb decisions but he's not stupid," Jackson said. "Or at least, he was lucky. He had the windows open, so . . . I guess he climbed out. Then he swam to shore."

"Still. That's so scary. I'm sorry," I said. "I'm glad he could swim to safety—he must not be too badly hurt. But why would he do that?"

"Beats me. When I called to check my messages there was one from him from earlier tonight—I guess I didn't hear my phone for a while. He'd called to tell me that he was 'jumping the ferry'—he has friends who live out there. I guess they were having a party." Jackson shook his head. "Anything for a party."

I pulled into the hospital parking lot and we took a spot in visitor parking, close to the building. As we hurried to the front door, I handed Jackson his keys—I had a feeling he'd be staying longer than I would.

His grandparents were inside, in the emergency room waiting area. Jackson went up to them to check in, and I followed, trailing slightly behind. "He's going to be fine, but they want to check him out. If anything, he needs to sober up," Jackson's grandfather was saying.

I wanted to meet all of them, but at the same time, I

didn't want to intrude on the family moment. "Call me later if you need anything," I said to Jackson, who was about to head into Franklin's room, then I made myself scarce.

I realized I was going to need a ride home, so I called Ava, but her phone went straight to voice mail. So I called Lucy and quickly explained the situation. She was more concerned about Franklin than I thought she would be. Then I realized: growing up together, she and Jackson had known each other's families. Of course.

"Everything's okay, but I need a favor. Can you come down here and pick me up?" I asked.

"Sure, of course," Lucy said. "Be there in ten minutes."

I sat on the curb and waited for her. And waited. And waited. I glanced at my watch. It had been at least half an hour by the time her red SUV pulled into the parking lot. She drove to the ER entrance and parked at the curb, lights flashing.

"Took you long enough," I said.

"You woke me up. I had to get dressed," she said.

I closed the door and clicked my seatbelt. "Sorry, I didn't mean to snap. I'm just super worried right now."

"You think I'm not? I can't imagine how Jackson's family is feeling right now," Lucy said. "Maybe I should go inside and see how everything is."

"I don't think there's anything we can do. They said he's fine."

"Maybe I wanted to see that for myself," she said quietly, as she revved the engine and peeled out of the parking lot.

"Okay, so you care about Jackson now, instead of hating him. I get it. But so do I," I said gently.

Lucy made a few turns and drove through town without saying another word. I didn't know what I could say, either.

We headed up the hill toward our house. "You just—how could you hook up with Jackson and then tell me *afterward*?" Lucy suddenly blurted out.

"I'm sorry," I said. "I know that wasn't the best way to go about it."

"Do you know how much that hurt?"

"But you weren't dating him. It's not like I betrayed you," I said.

"Yes, you did. Not because of anything you did with Jackson. That's irrelevant. But because you lied to me," she said. "You acted like you didn't even know him. You listened to me talk about how weird things were between us and how embarrassed I still felt sometimes. And then I saw you guys together, on the beach that night."

"What? When?"

"The night of the bonfire. I was looking for firewood

and first I saw him with someone, and then imagine my surprise—no, shock—when I saw it was *you*. Do you have any
idea how it felt to find out that way? It was like ten minutes
after you told me you knew him. Ten minutes after you pur-
posefully didn't mention he was the guy you liked."

I wanted to say that it hadn't been ten minutes, that it had
been hours later, but I was horrified she'd found out about
us that way. I'd had no idea she'd known anything before I
told her that morning. She must have hated me so much. She
must have wanted to interrupt me. "Why didn't you tell me
that night?" I asked. "Why didn't you say anything the next
morning when we talked?"

"I wanted to see how long it would take you, to see if
you were planning on telling me. To let it go that far—that
was—"

"But you have to listen to my side—everything happened
so fast, and I was trying not to hurt you," I said. "I didn't
want to make things harder for you than they were—"

"Do you realize how patronizing that sounds? No. You
were trying to do something behind my back and get away
with it, and make it easy on yourself—not me. You wanted
Jackson and you didn't care how that affected me," Lucy said.
"I invited you here this summer because you're my best friend.
But would one best friend really do that to another? Think

about it, Mikayla. If I did that to you, how would you feel?"

"I made a mistake," I said, starting to cry. "You've never done that? What do you want me to do? I don't want our summer to be like this. This wasn't the plan."

"You kind of ruined the plan," Lucy said.

"The plan *changed*," I responded. "What's so great about plans, anyway? Isn't it better when things just *happen*?"

"For all your talk about wanting to make sure I was okay with you seeing Jackson, you've made it pretty clear that you'd rather jeopardize our friendship than what you have with him. That you would deliberately withhold the truth if you thought it meant you'd get to date him. That's why I'm upset."

We pulled into the driveway. Lucy got out and slammed the car door. She started to walk toward the house, then she turned back. "I'll get some stuff and stay at my grandparents' tonight. I just don't know if I can be around you right now."

She strode into the house, leaving me standing there beside her car.

I stood in the driveway, brushing tears away. When I finally composed myself enough to enter the house, Lucy was barging out, overnight bag in hand.

"What's going on?" Ava asked from the doorway of the room we shared. She slipped off her headphones and walked out to meet me in the living room. "What is happening tonight?"

I sat down and told her about the accident, and Jackson, and how Lucy and I had argued in the car.

"Okay. This is getting ridiculous." Ava set down her water bottle on the coffee table. "Now you're here, Lucy's staying there . . . I'm stuck in the middle."

"Sorry," I said, clutching a pillow. "I wish you didn't have to be."

Ava ran her hands through her hair. "She's being ridiculous. Then again, so are you. I mean, you can't let a guy get in the way of your friendships. Ever. We covered this in Boyfriends 101."

"You keep referring to this imaginary course. I think I should have signed up for it." I laughed, despite how miserable I felt. "*He's* not in the way. She is. Or I am, or both. She's mad because I lied to her. And because our whole summer isn't going exactly according to plan."

"Plans are overrated," said Ava. "I mean, look how mine turned out. Supposed to be in Chicago having outrageous parties and watching the fireworks on Navy Pier tonight. Instead, I got my fortune told by the Viking Psychic and rather than finding love, like she promised, I'm watching a movie on my phone."

"I thought things might get a little better between me and Lucy as time went on, but they're actually getting worse," I admitted. "I don't know what to do to fix things. And I always fix things. That's my job."

"There's not much you can do, is there?" Ava asked.

Maybe there is, I thought. Maybe it was the only way to save this friendship.

CHAPTER 27

Lucy

I opened my eyes and saw a
curtain blowing in the breeze. A flouncy, lacy white curtain.
The kind we definitely didn't have at the cabin. For a minute
I had no idea where I was.

I rolled over and looked at the wall with its floral printed
wallpaper, and remembered I'd spent the night at my grandparents', in the guest room that used to be my mom's bedroom
when she was growing up. Now I was here, and she wasn't. It
was weird.

I checked my phone. Earlier the day before, Mom had
called to tell me she was headed home to the Twin Cities
to show some houses and to discuss all the wedding options
with Gary. That meant I could crash here without having to

go into detail with her about why. Actually, she hadn't called as often in the past couple of days.

I pulled a sweatshirt on over my T-shirt and pajama bottoms and shuffled downstairs to the kitchen. My grandfather was busy at the stove, while my grandmother was wiping down the counter.

"How were the fireworks last night?" She poured a cup of coffee and set it down in front of me.

That awful car ride with Mikayla flashed through my mind. "Um. Not what I'd thought they would be," I said.

"Oh? Did something happen?" she asked.

"What would happen?" I said, trying to keep things light. "I just needed some of your delicious breakfast. I was feeling a little homesick for you guys. I always stay here when I'm in town."

"Funny. I thought you liked having your own place," my grandfather said.

"I did. I mean, I do. Usually. But things are kind of weird right now," I admitted.

"Weird how?" He set down a small pitcher of maple syrup on the table.

Weird in that I didn't know how to get past the current situation. I'd finally come clean and told Mikayla that I wasn't okay with the way she'd gone about seeing Jackson.

I thought she would have been more apologetic, more sorry.

I didn't say anything and just sipped coffee. I figured if I let the comment die, they would too.

"Well, it's a gorgeous morning," Nana said. "How did you sleep?"

"Pretty good." I stretched my arms above my head and yawned. It was nice to have a place you could always go to when things got strange. My grandparents didn't change. They didn't break up, get remarried, leave town on whims or shopping sprees. They weren't interested in selling their own property or anyone else's. They were here for the orchard and farm, which weren't going anywhere.

"So. You going to tell us what's going on or should we drag it out of you, as per usual?" my grandmother asked.

"Why can't I just spend a night here with my favorite grandparents?" I asked.

"You can. Anytime. But you have these little worry lines by your mouth. Either you've taken up smoking and are getting premature wrinkles, or you're not feeling a hundred percent peachy."

"That would be weird," I said.

"What would?"

"Feeling peachy. Does that mean you're kind of mushy inside?"

"Sweet and sunny," said my grandfather.

"Ew," my grandmother and I said at the same time. "That's over the top," Nana said, "even for you."

"So is taking up smoking," I said. "Why would I do that now? Or ever? And I don't have worry lines, I just got up and I'm tired!" I said. "Everything's fine."

"Right. And I suppose you don't want any flapjacks."

"Pretty please?" I clasped my hands together and looked up at him.

He stood above me with the spatula holding two fresh pancakes. "Tell us what's going on and we'll feed you."

"That sounds like really strange blackmail."

"Yes, I know. I suppose I can't hold flapjacks hostage." Grandpa set the pancakes on my plate. "If you don't feel like talking right now, it's okay. But you know that you can."

"Thanks." I nodded and poured some syrup. Was it weird that I didn't want to confide in them about Mikayla? How would my grandparents look at me if I told them about this whole situation? My grandmother already thought I was ridiculous for being upset that she'd hired Jackson, back when I first showed up. She didn't see why we couldn't be friends; she wouldn't understand now, either.

"One last question. Is it about your mother?" Nana asked. "I know Kerri was driving you crazy with her wedding plans."

"No, it's not that," I said. "Though she is going over the top with everything. Even the napkins. How did she *get* like that? You guys are so laid-back most of the time."

My grandparents looked at each other and shrugged. "The apple does in fact fall far from the tree?" Nana guessed.

"Try to cut her a break," Grandpa added. "She means well and she loves you to pieces. She just can't help herself." He walked out of the room for a minute and I cornered my nana.

"Okay. I'll tell you one thing," I said. "But you have to promise to keep it to yourself."

"Sure. What's that?"

"I kind of like someone—"

"Jackson?" she asked.

"*No!* Not Jackson. Someone else," I said. "But I'm totally afraid to find out if he feels the same way."

"Why?"

"What if he doesn't?" I said. "And I make a total fool out of myself?" *Again*, I added silently, *the way I did with Jackson.*

"But what if he *does*?" Nana countered. "Why don't you think about it that way?"

"Because I'm not a positive person when it comes to stuff like this?"

"You're only seventeen. I think you can change your tune."

My forehead creased as I thought about it. "I don't have a tune."

"You *know* what I mean," she said. "Now quit hanging around here, go get dressed, and get back out there. Is it anyone I know?"

I shook my head. "Not yet, anyway."

"See?" She nodded, smiling. "Now you're talking."

CHAPTER 28

Mikayla

Jackson walked out onto the deck on the back of our house, where I was hanging out on Saturday night. He slouched against the doorway. He looked as devastatingly cute as usual. "What's going on?" he asked.

"What are you doing here? You can't be here," I said, setting down my book. We had to leave the cabin before Lucy showed up. Where was she, anyway? It was nearly seven. I'd been home for an hour already, waiting for her. I hadn't seen her since our fight two nights ago—she'd been staying at her grandparents'. I was ready to talk about things again. I wanted to tell her what I'd decided. I wondered if she just planned on avoiding me for the rest of the summer by staying at her grandparents'.

"Why can't I be here?" He came a little bit closer and perched on an arm of the chair, looking down at me. "What's going on with *you*? You've been avoiding me. I sent you a dozen texts. I called. I even looked for you at work, on my lunch hour," Jackson said.

"I was out on a mini golf and alpine slide adventure today," I said. "You should have seen the kids. Jeremy was in heaven."

Jackson looked at me like that wasn't the answer he wanted to hear. "What did I do?" he asked. "Did I do something wrong?"

I shook my head. "No, it's not you."

"Then what is it? I haven't seen you since the night of the carnival and—and Franklin's accident."

"How's he doing, by the way?" I asked.

"Not too bad. He's back home in Saint Paul and my parents are working to get him signed up for a few things—like rehab, maybe. He's probably going to be charged with reckless driving, but at least he only crashed into a lake. So it's not as serious as it could have been, in lots of ways, I guess. I mean, at least he didn't hurt someone else. That would have been the worst."

I nodded. "I'm glad he's okay."

"Me too. But getting back to you," Jackson said. He reached for a curl of my hair and tugged gently on it.

"We should go somewhere," I blurted, getting up and stepping away from him.

"Why?"

"Because Lucy will come home and it'll be weird. Come on," I said. "Let's go for a walk."

"Lucy's not the one who's being weird right now," Jackson said as he followed me off the deck and through the house to the front door.

I ignored his comment as I slipped on my flip-flops and we headed outside. "Let's drive somewhere," I said.

"If I do, will you tell me what's going on?" said Jackson. I nodded yes, and we got into his Jetta.

The problem was that I didn't know where to go, exactly. I needed somewhere we could have a private conversation—and someplace I could get back from without needing a car. Things might not end well.

Jackson started the engine and pulled out of the driveway. "Where should I go?" he asked.

"I don't know," I said. "A park?"

"Fine," Jackson said, shifting gears a little too aggressively. About five minutes later, he pulled into the parking lot of a small town park. He switched off the engine and turned to me. "So."

"So." I fiddled with the window switch, rolling it up and

down a few times. Should I tell him what was going on with Lucy? If I did, it would explain things. But it would also be sharing information I was pretty sure Lucy wouldn't want me to share. "I really like hanging out with you. I think you know that," I began.

"Uh-oh. This is going to be one of *those* conversations."

"What do you mean?"

"Never mind." Jackson shook his head. "Go on."

"I just feel like we moved too fast. I need to slow things down," I said.

"What do you mean? We didn't move too fast," Jackson said.

"But we don't know each other that well and we're spending all our spare time together, and—"

"Is that a problem?" he asked. "I thought that's what you wanted—what we both wanted."

"It is," I said. "But—I don't know how to explain this. I just need some time on my own."

"Is this, like, something we're going to get over?" Jackson asked. "Or not?"

We were both silent for a minute. I didn't know what to say. I wanted to slide across the car seat to Jackson and hug him and tell him everything was going to be okay. But I couldn't get that close to him, knowing how mad it made Lucy.

"I just don't think we can hang out all the time. I think we should take a break," I told Jackson.

"I don't get you. Two days ago everything was fine. Now all of a sudden you—you're breaking up with me?" Jackson said. "What did I do?"

I hated having to hurt his feelings like this. He was assuming he was the problem, when he wasn't. But there was no way I'd betray Lucy's trust and tell him the whole story. That wasn't my story to tell, anyway.

"You didn't do anything! I still—" I stopped myself before I finished the sentence. *Still want to be friends.*

"I don't know why you're doing this. Come on, don't do this. Whatever's going on, we can work it out." Jackson scooted closer to me. He laced his fingers through mine and squeezed. "I can't imagine the rest of the summer without hanging out with you." He reached out to touch my face, and gently pulled me closer. "I'm, like . . . I don't know what I'd do without you." He started to kiss me, and although I'd sworn I'd keep my distance, I kissed him back. We moved closer and closer to each other and I gave in to my emotions for a second. I wanted to stay in his arms forever. I wanted to snuggle close to him, as close as two people could get.

I put my hand on his chest and pulled back. "No. I feel the exact same way, Jackson. But I can't be with you."

"I'll go away if you really want me to. But you can't say we don't have chemistry," Jackson said, trying to kiss me again.

I backed up a little. "No, we—I can't. I need a break."

I would never have imagined that I would be pushing away a guy as wonderful as Jackson. Maybe it would turn out to be a big mistake and I'd lose him for good. Maybe I would never have another boyfriend, ever. I wasn't good at this stuff—at all. But I was learning. Friends came first. They always had, and they always should.

CHAPTER 29

Lucy

I stood on the shore of Lake Superior on Saturday after work, next to a couple of sea kayaks, and looked out at the water. Over the years, I'd heard many stories about how dangerous the lake could be—from my grandparents, my mother, even people at home who'd had intense experiences while on vacation here. I'd heard the expression "The lake is boss."

"I thought Claire was meeting us," I said to Gus.

"She texted to say she can't make it. Someone called in sick so she's working tonight," Gus said.

"Oh? Too bad." Honestly, I didn't know whether I was disappointed by the news—or excited. I was counting on her to be there in case things got weird or intense. I took out my phone. Her text must have come while I was driving. It said *Have fun tonight!* with a little smiley face emoticon.

I was feeling a little nervous about this turn of events, but I wasn't going to back out now. So this wasn't the original plan we'd made when Gus called earlier that day. As Mikayla had told me: Isn't life better when things just happen, instead of being planned? You can't plan everything.

So, fine. Here I was, giving her theory a shot.

As much as I'd been trying to not feel something for Gus, I found that when I was at work every day, I spent a ridiculous amount of time wishing he would drop by. Ever since I'd run off on the Fourth of July, I'd been regretting my choice, and I wasn't about to make the same mistake twice.

"I can't believe you talked me into doing this," I said. "I thought this was only for experienced kayakers."

"I am experienced. I'm leading the tour," Gus said. He was making a few adjustments to his kayak and stowing things in the back hatch—a compartment where you can put supplies you need to keep dry. He pulled the cover over the hatch.

"You just got the job two days ago," I said. "Now all of a sudden you're experienced?"

"I only got the job because I've done a lot of kayaking, dummy," he teased, handing me a paddle.

"Um, your lessons leave a little bit to be desired." I hadn't been out on the big lake in a sea kayak. It was a lot different—and a lot more frightening—than kayaking anywhere else. Right now the lake looked calm, but I'd been out on it on a ferry one time when it changed, and suddenly there were big waves that sent the boat up high and then crashing down. How would I handle that in a teeny tiny kayak, on my own?

"Here, read this," Gus said, handing me a brochure from the kayak and canoe rental company where he was now employed.

TOP FIVE THINGS TO REMEMBER:

Enjoy the sea caves, sandstone cliffs, lighthouses, islands, and sea stacks.

Conditions can change in an instant. Be prepared. Plan your trip accordingly.

Lake Superior is never warmer than 50 degrees. If you fall in or capsize, hypothermia is imminent.

You cannot go ashore in several areas. Be aware of this.

Bears are excellent swimmers and can be found on all of the islands.

Great. Why was I doing this again? Gus had called the store and insisted that we go on "a paddle," but for me it was more about survival.

"Bears?" I said. "Since when do the islands have bears?"

"They probably always have. Don't worry, we're not planning to camp," Gus said.

"That's what you say now, but it says here, number two, that conditions can change in an instant."

"The lake is really calm right now, and I have a backup plan," Gus said. "Trust me."

I smiled nervously as I got into the boat, and Gus pulled the spray skirt—the thing that keeps water from getting into the kayak and freezing your legs—over the cockpit. He handed me my paddle and then gave me a gentle push away from dock. I balanced the long paddle, getting used to the feel of it, while he caught up with me. I bobbed on the gentle waves, adjusting to being on the water.

"We'll go along the shore, check out some of the sea caves," Gus said. "Then we can head to Latchkey Island, which is just right over there. Not far at all. I brought some food, so we can have a little picnic and head back before sunset."

"Why am I not surprised? Are you always going to bring food?" I asked.

"Probably."

I'd said *always* as if we were a couple or something. Which we weren't. "Not that I'm complaining!" I said. "Because by the time we get there I have a feeling I'm going to be starving." My arms were in better shape than they had been at the start of the summer, but still, paddling wasn't something I'd done much of this year. I knew that trying to keep up with Gus would probably mean I'd shred my muscles before long. But I had to keep up. I wasn't sure exactly why I had to, but I did.

There were so many things to see: rocks, sea caves, birds, lighthouses, sailboats, and other kayakers like us. This was the perfect summer day to be out on the water and I'd probably never have done it without Gus. I'd been staying inside way too much and not doing half the things I meant to do. He was getting me out of a rut.

"What should I do?" I yelled to Gus, who was trying to paddle over to me, but the waves kept pushing him back.

The wind had come up and gotten heavier; darker clouds seemed to be just sitting on the horizon. Actually, more like right above our heads. Threatening to dump rain at any second. We'd been kayaking for a little over two hours, and it had been going so well that we'd gone a little farther than we planned. But just as we'd turned to head back, the weather had turned as well—and so had the lake. It was looking evil and shipwreck-ish.

"We're too far from shore to get there safely!" Gus yelled back.

Great. That wasn't what I wanted to hear.

"I mean, we could make it—but let's not risk it. Let's try for Latchkey Island!" Gus shouted.

I didn't like how he used the word *try*. It implied we might not make it. I wanted to look in the direction Gus was pointing, but I didn't dare take my eyes off the water.

The bow of my kayak seemed to be pointed straight up at the sky. Then the lake heaved with a big wave, and the bow tilted straight down, so that the stern was up. This was like a really bad amusement park ride that I couldn't wait to get off.

I pushed thoughts of nausea out of my mind and focused, using every last ounce of strength I had. Finally I glimpsed a small, rocky beach. We half surfed and half coasted onto it. Gus jumped out and stubbed his toes; when I tried to get out of my kayak, I lost my balance, slipped, and fell right into the lake.

"You okay?" Gus reached out to help me up, gripping my

hand tightly. I slipped and fell against him, teetering to catch my balance. "Whoa. Sea legs can really mess you up."

"I guess," I admitted, feeling very unsteady. We stood there, just breathing hard for a second, right next to each other. "Wow. I can't believe we just went through that."

"It was intense," Gus agreed. "But you weren't worried, were you? I mean, I had everything under control."

"Maybe you did. But I'm not sure I did." We both started laughing. "Did you *see* that one giant wave?"

"I thought you were going over. For sure," Gus said.

We dragged our boats up onto the beach and Gus grabbed a bag out of one of the hatches on his kayak. He pulled out a water bottle and handed it to me.

"I can barely lift my arms to drink this." I took a few gulps and felt the adrenaline coursing through me start to lessen a bit. I handed the bottle to him and watched as he had some. What was so interesting about watching him do simple stuff? I didn't get it, but it seemed like he knew how to do everything really, really well. I liked that about him.

Gus wiped the water off his mouth with his arm and caught me staring at him.

"So," I cleared my throat. "What do we do now?"

"It really depends on a lot of things. Sometimes the waves quiet down in the evening. If they do, we'll hurry back. But, if that doesn't happen, or it gets dark before that happens, we might have to wait until morning."

"Morning? I'm going to miss work."

"Maybe. Maybe we'll get back in time, though. I think you should forget about work. Just relax and try to enjoy this." Gus shrugged.

"But where are we going to—sleep?" I asked.

"I'm prepared," Gus said. He coughed, like he'd just said the wrong thing. "I mean, uh, I have emergency supplies. I have a plastic tarp we can sleep under; I have a microfleece blanket. We just have to hope it doesn't get too cold tonight, because it's not that thick of a blanket."

"Do you have that terrible freeze-dried camping food?"

"No, just water, grapes, some cheese, and some candy bars."

"There's no way we can contact anyone. Is there? I didn't even bring my phone. I didn't want it to get wet."

"I have mine. Don't worry. Who did you want to call?" Gus asked.

"I don't know. The coast guard?" I joked. Well, sort of half joked. I wouldn't mind being rescued.

Gus took his phone out and peered at the screen. "Huh. That's weird. No bars. Okay, so we won't call anyone. But we're perfectly fine. Nothing's going to happen to us. We'll just wait for calmer waters."

◆◆◆

Two hours later, we were still waiting. The wind had let up a little, but the lake was still choppy—too rough for us to head back, especially because it was starting to get dark. The time had gone quickly because we'd played cards (Mr. Prepared even had those in his emergency kit) and talked about everything under the sun.

We'd eaten all the food, but were saving the water. Thanks to my falling out of the kayak and into the lake, I was shivering. Gus set up the blue tarp so that it arced over two tree branches.

"There's only one thing left to do," he said.

"What. Start a fire?" I asked, rubbing my arms.

"No. It's too windy," he said. "Get under the blanket." He sat down under the tarp, put the blanket over his legs and gestured for me to join him.

"Really?" I asked. "But it's only nine thirty. We just like . . . go to sleep?"

"We'll get warm, and then if we *can* sleep, yeah," he said. "Have you really never gone camping?"

"Of course I have," I said. It's just that I usually had a real tent and a sleeping bag, and I didn't usually share it with a boy.

"So come over here. I won't bite," Gus said. "Much."

"Ha ha," I said, narrowing my eyes as I crouched down and sat beside him. He spread the black fleece blanket over both of us, covering our legs and tucking it around our shoulders so that our hands would be covered. The blanket wasn't quite big enough for two people. We really had to be right up against each other for it to cover us.

It felt bizarre to be right next to him. His shirt smelled like sunscreen, the kind I usually used. Wait. Maybe it was my sunscreen. We were so close I couldn't tell.

"You know, maybe if you quit your job, and I quit mine, we could just spend the summer kayaking and camping," Gus said.

"'Cause this is working out so well for us?" I asked, smiling at him.

"Hey, if we'd planned to camp out, we would have done it totally right. But it's still working out. I just don't like the fact that you're cold."

"I'm . . . warming up," I said. *You have no idea how much.* "I still don't think I'd quit my job. No offense. I need the money."

"Oh, you're working in apples for the *money.* I thought you were doing it for the prestige," he said.

"Shut up." I elbowed him in the ribs. "And it's very prestigious. Just try to get a job there. You'll find out."

"I did. It was taken already." He snuggled under the blanket, moving a little closer to me.

"Oh." Well, that was awkward. "Sorry."

"It's okay. I found out they were hiring from within. Although how does that apply to Jackson?" Gus asked.

"We knew each other when we were kids. We were neighbors. And then, well, actually it was more that my grandparents know his grandparents." I sipped my water, not sure what to say next. Should I go into the whole history with Jackson? Should I tell him what had happened with Mikayla? I was enjoying being away from all that, and thinking about other things. "So. Are we going to sit up all night, or can we lie down?" As soon as the words were out of my mouth, I think my face must have turned a hundred shades of pink. That sounded so forward of me! I hoped he didn't take it the wrong way. Then again, it was Gus. He wasn't like that.

I stretched out on the ground and pulled the blanket more tightly around my shoulders. He did the same, shifting to get comfortable. We were using our life jackets for pillows. "This is a great hotel," Gus said. "They left pine needles on my pillow."

I laughed. "Are there really black bears here?" I asked.

"Nope," Gus said.

"Phew."

"But there are brown bears."

"Very funny."

"I'm just telling the truth!" Gus shrugged. "If you happen to see one? Just act natural."

"What does that mean?" I asked, laughing. "Be all casual? 'Hey, Bear. How's it going, dude?'"

Gus laughed too. "Since we don't have any food left, I'm not worried."

"On the plus side," I murmured.

"On the plus side," he agreed.

My body was so exhausted from the long paddle to the island. I'm not sure when it happened, but at some point I leaned against Gus and fell asleep. I woke up a couple of times in the middle of the night. The first time I woke up, Gus was lying on his back, and my head was resting on his chest. I immediately sat up, looking around, trying to figure out where I was.

"You okay?" Gus asked, sitting up and rubbing his eyes. "Lucy?"

I'm here with Gus? I wasn't sure if this was real or not. "Yeah. I'm—I'm fine."

"Warm enough?" he asked, scooting back under the blanket.

I nodded, snuggling back against him. "Perfect."

The next time I woke up, we were lying beside each other, spooning. I was so excited by what seemed to be happening that I couldn't fall back asleep for a long time.

CHAPTER 30

Mikayla

"What are you doing here?" Ava greeted me when I walked into the Blackbird Café a few hours after my conversation with Jackson Saturday night.

"I tried calling but you never picked up. Then I tried calling the café and that didn't work very well either. Now I know why." The restaurant was almost totally full, and a band was performing in the bar area, singing a cover of a song that I thought was by Pearl Jam, one of my parents' favorite bands.

Ava led me over to a small table just outside the bar area. "What's going on?" she asked.

"I'm worried about Lucy. I've been waiting for her to come back to the house so we can talk, but she hasn't showed. I tried calling her, and the phone started ringing. In her room. I went in and it was on her dresser, next to her wallet. After I couldn't reach you, I texted Claire. The last thing she knew, Lucy was headed out kayaking with Gus."

"So . . . maybe this is a *good* thing she's not home yet, not a bad thing?" Ava said.

"Maybe. I knew she liked him." I hoped that Lucy and Gus were just having fun together and staying out late doing something after the kayak trip. Then again . . . what if they had run into trouble? "On the other hand, it's been dark for a couple of hours. If they're still on the water . . . that's a problem."

Ava glanced around the restaurant. "I just need to make sure my tables don't need anything. Be right back."

I listened to the band and texted my mom, then sent her a picture of the lead singer. She'd be happy that I was out listening to music on a Saturday night. I thought about Jackson and wondered what he was doing right now. Breaking up with him had been nearly impossible. Still, for the first time since I'd learned his name, I didn't feel like I was being a bad friend. That had to count for something.

"Here." Ava delivered a tall glass of lemonade to my table. "This way they can't accuse me of stealing a table.

You're a paying customer. So what can we do? Should we try to get in touch with Gus?"

"I don't want to interfere . . . I'd just like to know she's okay. I was really hoping to talk with her tonight, to work things out." I sipped the lemonade. Not that I knew what I was going to say, but I was going to try. Losing Lucy's friendship wasn't part of *any* scenario I had in mind.

"Speaking of being in charge. Assuming she gets back tonight . . . I think we really need to have a house meeting tomorrow," Ava said. "In fact, I'm calling one. Right now."

"We do?"

"We do," Ava said. "I *want* to have a party next weekend. We are going to have a party. And we can't do it when you guys are having your little feud. See that singer over there? I want to invite him. But I can't if we don't have this party. Back before school got out, that's all you guys talked about: how great this summer would be, and how you were going to be so independent and have your own place and people would come over . . ."

"I know," I said. "That was the plan. Even though things have changed, and I never imagined I'd be in this situation right now, I still want all those things. And I want all of us to have a great summer together," I said. "That's why I broke up with Jackson tonight. It just isn't going to work out, and I'd rather be sad now than see Lucy miserable."

"What? You broke up with him?" Ava asked. "But you guys—you're really good together, it seems like."

"I know, but . . . if it upsets Lucy that much, I have to," I said.

"I did *not* cover breaking up in Boyfriends 101 yet. You should have talked to me about it first," Ava said.

"It's not funny," I said, wiping away a tear.

"Oh, no. No, it's not funny. I'm sorry, I was just trying to lighten things up." Ava leaned over and gave me a hug. "So how did he take it?"

"Not that well," I said. "But, it's done. I guess." I let out a long, shuddery sigh.

"Aw, that's sad. I can't stand it when *both* you guys are sad. Listen, I have to get back to work, but stick around for a while. I'll be off in an hour," Ava said, getting up to respond to a customer waving at her.

I waited for a few minutes, then got up and went outside into the cool night air. I unlocked my bike from the street sign outside the café and started riding back to the house. If I was going to cry, I wanted to do it in private.

I glanced up at the night sky, still in awe at how many stars I could see in Bridgeport. It was a clear night, so even if

Lucy and Gus were still on the lake—which I couldn't imagine—they wouldn't be in danger of any storms.

Wherever Lucy was, I hoped she was okay. I'd done what I could do to make things right. Now it was her move.

CHAPTER 31

Lucy

Gus and I stood on the wooden dock outside the kayak shop in the bright morning sunshine. I felt kind of awkward, my legs a little wobbly, like I'd been on the water too long and wasn't sure how to walk on land.

When I'd woken up that morning, Gus wasn't lying beside me any more—he was busy getting the boats ready for our trip back across the bay. In a way, I was relieved—I wasn't sure how to act when I woke up next to a guy without having a toothbrush around. We'd said good morning and talked a little bit about how hungry we felt, but other than that, all business. I wondered if he felt as embarrassed as I did about snuggling the night before. Nothing had happened, technically, but I'd definitely never felt that close to a guy. Ever. Ever ever ever.

Now Gus was cleaning out the boats and getting them ready to stow in the racks by the store. I helped carry them over, and then brought the paddles, life jackets, and spray skirts into the store.

We went back outside, and I wasn't sure what came next. I picked up my backpack from the docks. "So, I should get going—I have to run to work. Thanks for a great trip. You can chop almonds well, and you can paddle through choppy water. Big points in the chop department."

"That sounds weird," he said.

"I am weird," I said, kicking at a rock. "Sorry."

"It's okay. I like you anyway," he said. "Or maybe I like you because you're weird. Have you thought of that?" He stepped closer to me.

He's going to kiss me, I suddenly realized. "So, I'll see you later," I said, backing up toward my car. The easiest thing to do here was to just stay friends. Nothing more. Maybe the night before I'd felt differently, like I could be close to Gus, maybe even put my fears to rest and just go for it, but in the glaring light this morning I couldn't handle it.

"Can I ask you something?" Gus said. "Didn't something sort of happen between us last night? I mean, I thought you and I . . . we kind of had a connection."

"We did," I said, glancing at him and then looking away. We'd bonded over surviving on grapes and Snickers bars. We'd snuggled under a blanket. I got shivers, the good kind of shivers, thinking about it—not that I could tell Gus that.

"Why don't we still have one?" Gus asked. "Because that was only twelve hours ago, and right now it kind of feels like you're running away from me."

"I guess . . . I have a hard time trusting people. After a bunch of things that have happened," I said. "I know we get along okay. But, like, at any minute, something could change. You might not be up-front with me all the time."

"What would I possibly be hiding from you? I tell you everything," Gus said.

"But I don't know that," I said. "Do I? How could I know that?"

"Because I'm being honest—aren't you?"

"Well . . . yeah," I said. "Of course I am!"

"So why wouldn't I be? I don't have a secret life. I barely have a life, period. Wait, I shouldn't say that out loud, should I?" Gus asked. "In case you can't tell, I like hanging out with you. We have fun, and I . . . would like to be more. But . . . you know. If you're not interested then I guess we shouldn't hang out. Because it's too awkward."

But . . . I am interested, I wanted to say. *I'm actually a little bit crazy about you.*

He walked off toward the kayak shop, and I stood there feeling stuck. He was asking me to take a bungee jump and trust that the line wouldn't break.

I rushed back to the cabin, showered, and changed. When I grabbed my phone, I saw several texts—apparently everyone had been wondering where I was. It wasn't like me to just be gone. There was even a text from Mikayla, begging me to let her know I got the message and that I was okay.

I sent a group text explaining what had happened, then got to work as quickly as I could. I was rearranging and dusting the mugs when I picked up one that had an image of a sea cave on it. I thought about how Gus and I had kayaked through them, how when I was out on the water with him I felt like my summer up here was finally starting. Then I'd blown it. Making it the shortest summer on record.

Suddenly the mug slipped from my hand and it crashed to the tile floor, shattering into a dozen pieces. "Agh!" I cried. "Why do I have to ruin everything?"

"Hey. Don't sweat it. It's just a mug," Jackson said, coming over to me. "I'll get the broom. It's no big deal."

"It's not the stupid mug," I said. "It's me! I'm such an idiot sometimes."

"What's going on?" asked Jackson. He crouched down with a small whisk broom and dustpan and started sweeping up the mug shards.

"What do you care?" I replied, looking down at him.

He whisked the pieces of stoneware into the dustpan. "I do care. What, do you think I'm heartless?" He walked behind the counter and dumped the mess into the trash.

"Sometimes," I mumbled.

Jackson walked over to the store doors and put the little round red-apple clock with the *I will return at . . .* message on the door. A tourist walking toward the store came to a dead stop on the sidewalk, with a confused expression.

"Listen. Just because I happened to fall for your best friend—that doesn't make me heartless. I didn't know she was your friend! I hardly knew anything about you anymore, considering you hadn't talked to me in years—"

"What? *You* never spoke to *me*," I said.

He ignored that and kept on going. "Now you and I have been getting along, but you're still mad at me, and instead of talking about it with me—you're taking it out on Mikayla."

"What? No, I'm not," I said.

"I think you are." Jackson hoisted himself onto the counter and sat facing me.

I fiddled with the postcards, not sure what to say. I was

glad he was sorry. But I had to explain why it had hurt me so much. I didn't talk about stuff like this—not often, anyway. "It was awkward," I said. "Really awkward. Not just because we were friends and I ruined that—"

"Maybe you didn't," he said. "Maybe it was just the fact we both changed schools."

"Yeah, but—" I laughed nervously. "I tried to kiss you."

Jackson shrugged. "So . . . yeah. You did."

"And you couldn't get away from me fast enough," I said.

He grabbed the basket of magnets on the counter and started sifting through it. "I just didn't want it to be like that. We were friends. That's all I, like, wanted back then."

"Yeah," I said, "I *know*." I laughed again. "I found that out. And you know what? I was really just acting on impulse that day. It wasn't something I planned. It was embarrassing, sure, but I could have dealt with that. I don't like you that way now. You know that, right?"

"Um, yeah. That's obvious. It always has been," he said. "You hardly like me at all."

"I do, but the issue with you—why I couldn't forgive you—it isn't that dumb kiss. It's because you humiliated me when you told everyone at school how I was in love with you, and how embarrassing it was for me because you blew me off, and how I fell apart and started crying, and wasn't that sad—"

"What? Whoa, whoa. I never said that!" Jackson cried.

"Then what did you say?" I asked him.

"I didn't know what to do. So I asked Owen for advice," Jackson said, naming a friend who'd been in our group. "I didn't want to be mean to you, and I wanted to stay friends, at least until the end of the school year when we all moved on. I wanted to know how to do that."

"It wouldn't have been that hard, we just would have kept our distance," I said.

"Sure, I can see that now. Back then? I was clueless about girls. I think I told Owen you seemed kind of surprised or upset by my reaction. He made up the story from there," Jackson said. "When I heard the rumor, I tried to change the story, but it was too late. Everyone had *his* version. He added in things like how you were crying. That *wasn't* me."

"Oh. Well, good." I hadn't seen Owen in three years. If I ever saw him again, I'd just punch him in the nose. "So can you kind of see why I hated you?"

Jackson nodded.

"I have the hardest time trusting people. I know it's not your fault," I said. "I just do. It's the way my parents told me they were getting divorced, it's eighth grade, it's a whole bunch of things. So when I found out about you and Mikayla before she even told me about you guys . . . that really hurt.

That I felt I couldn't trust her to just be honest with me."

"But I—we—didn't know. I only found out she knew you the night of the bonfire," Jackson said.

"Yeah, I get that now," I said. "I had some time to think while I was stranded on an island last night with Gus."

"Is there a story?" Jackson asked.

"The only story is that I screwed things up when we got back," I said. "Because I can't trust him."

"Here's my theory: You should just assume you can trust people until they prove otherwise. Otherwise you're constantly looking for problems when they're not there. And then you're the problem," Jackson said.

"Like you know me that well. You haven't even seen me for three years—"

"I'm not talking about *you*," Jackson said. "I'm talking about me, too. Ever since my brother started lying to us about everything, I have a really hard time believing anything anyone says. But I have to remind myself it's *not* everyone. Just him."

"Sorry."

"And Gus is not a liar. He's a completely decent guy. And maybe you don't want to hear this right now, but so is Mikayla."

"No, she's not," I said.

"She is," Jackson insisted.

"I meant she's not a guy," I said.

Jackson narrowed his eyes. "Very funny. Think of everything you know about her. I mean, you know her way better than I do, but come on: She is about the most innocent and honest person ever. Which is why it really sucks that she gave me the let's-just-be-friends talk last night."

"What?" I asked.

"She broke up with me," Jackson said. "She said things moved too quickly, and she needed more time to herself."

"I had no idea . . . I haven't seen her in a day or two." Here I'd been blaming Mikayla for my problems, assuming she was having the dream summer while I was moping around being jealous and miserable.

It was in reverse. I'd just spent the night with Gus—a fun, exciting, though slightly worrisome night—while she was having an awful time. I'd bet anything she broke up with Jackson because I refused to forgive her. That was the message I'd been giving her.

I needed to talk to her instead of ignoring her. "I'll find her right after work and see how she's doing. Maybe if she knows I'm okay with you guys seeing each other, she'll change her mind. I know how much she likes you," I said. "This is probably all my fault and nothing to do with you."

"Can you do it any sooner than after work?" he asked, sliding off the counter. "And don't worry about Gus. He really likes you, I told you."

"Yeah, but can you guarantee—"

"Nope. No guarantees," Jackson said. The doorbell for the back door rang, which usually meant a truck delivery. Jackson left to go sign for it, and I sat down behind the counter. I pulled the gift basket from Gus out from underneath the counter and opened a bag of chocolate-covered pretzels.

I started eating absentmindedly while I thought about it. The trust thing had been my problem for a while now. In fact, I'd always kept the people I really trusted—like Ava and Mikayla—really close. It took me a long time to feel comfortable trusting anyone. So didn't it make sense that it killed me when I found out I couldn't?

I was angry with Mikayla because she'd proved me right: that no one could be trusted.

She could be trusted, though. In almost every situation we'd ever run into—until now. She had told me about Jackson, as soon as something had happened.

I'd overreacted. I needed to make things right—with a few people.

◆◆◆

I begged Grandpa to let me out of work early so I could go find Gus and get the rest of my plan started. I drove to the kayak shop and parked around the side. I felt like I was spying as I quietly entered the busy shop.

I edged around the display units, looking for Gus. I could hear him laughing and, when I followed the noise, saw him hanging out with a few coworkers. He was working behind the rental counter, doing paperwork. He didn't notice me, so I crouched down. I was stalling. Big-time. If I knew what I wanted to do, then why was it so hard to actually just do it?

I walked past the shelves and displays of accessories and hid in the racks of wet suits for sale, waiting until I got my nerve up to go talk to him. I picked up a couple of canoeing guides and leafed through them while I listened to him joke around and even sing a little while he told a story, making his friends crack up.

There might be a side to him that I didn't know yet. That weird singing side. And I'd have to look at that as intriguing, instead of worrying.

You can do that, I told myself.

I walked up to the counter and put a canoeing guide on the counter in front of him. "You rent canoes, right?"

"Uh, actually, yes, we do," he stuttered.

"Because I need to rent a canoe. For tomorrow. And I

need a guide," I said. "Preferably someone who's, like, a veteran canoe-er."

"Canoeist," Gus said. "We're called canoeists."

"And I want someone who's not going to correct everything I say. Plus, it'd be nice to have a catered lunch. Do you offer that?"

Gus glanced at his coworkers, who were staring at us like we were acting completely weird. "Uh, maybe we should step over here so we can go over all the options," Gus said. He gestured for me to join him by the back door, then we ran outside, laughing.

"I can be that person," Gus said.

"Good." I leaned into him and kissed him firmly on the lips. It might not have been smooth or dramatic, but I definitely got my point across. I gently pushed him with my body and he pushed me back, until we were right up against the building.

"Wow. I've never made out at work before," Gus said, when we finally separated.

"Me . . . neither?" I said as he curled my hair around my ear and ran his finger down my cheek.

"I should probably be getting back inside," he said.

I nodded, feeling breathless. "Probably. Do you want to meet up later?" I asked.

"When later?" His hands were resting on my waist.

"I'm not sure. It might be really late. It might be tomorrow," I said.

"I think tonight is a better idea," he said.

"Okay. But first can you help me make a gourmet picnic?" I asked.

"That depends. Am I invited?"

"Not this time. But I promise we'll spend lots of picnics together."

CHAPTER 32

Mikayla

My Club walkie-talkie beeped just as I was putting away the badminton rackets.

"It's Liam at the front gate. Someone here to see you. Needs verbal permission to come in as a guest."

My heart pounded—half from fear and half from excitement. Jackson? But no, everyone here knew him—even Liam would let him in without a fuss. "Who is it?" I asked.

"Lucy Carpenter," Liam said brusquely. "You know her?"

"Of—of course I know her," I said. "You even know that, Liam. *You* know her. From the bonfire, at least."

"Maybe you're right, but that doesn't settle anything. The question is if *you* approve of letting her in to see you," he said.

I quickly gave Liam the okay to admit Lucy, surprised he

didn't want it written in blood, then rushed through getting everything stowed. *If she's here to see me, that's good. Unless she shows up with all my stuff in her car.* I hurried to visitor parking in front of the main club building. My pulse quickened as I saw Lucy getting out of her little red SUV.

"Hey," she said.

"Hi," I said.

"Uh, do you have plans tonight?" she asked.

I shook my head. "No, not at all—I'm done here as soon as I go check out."

"Cool." Lucy curled a lock of hair around her ear. "Do you think you could come with me to get Ava?"

"Of course. Is she okay? Where are we going?" I asked.

"She's fine, and it's a surprise. Kind of," she said.

"Okay, I'll be right back," I told her, hoping it was the good kind of surprise and not the bad kind.

I hurried to sign out, turned in my walkie-talkie for the night, and grabbed my bag from my locker. I'd leave my bike locked to the rack and figure that part out later. If Lucy was in a forgiving mood, I wasn't going to put up any roadblocks. What if something I did made her change her mind?

Our ride to the Blackbird was silent and awkward. I made occasional comments about the traffic or the weather. Lucy commented a bit in reply, but that was it. I felt like I was talking to a distant cousin instead of one of my best friends. "Does she know we're coming?" I asked as Lucy pulled into a fifteen-minute parking spot in front of the café.

She nodded. "She should be out here any second."

We sat listening to the radio, windows open. I drummed my fingers on the door, wondering when Lucy would tell me what this was all about. I wanted to think that she had come to get us in order to make things better, but I was almost afraid to get *too* hopeful.

A minute later, Ava came dashing out of the Blackbird Café, purse tucked under her arm. She looked furtive, glancing over her shoulder a few times as if she was running away. She spotted the car and hurried toward us. When she climbed into the backseat, she slammed the door behind her. "Take off!" she told Lucy. "Take off now."

"Are you in trouble or something?" Lucy asked, checking the side mirror as she pulled onto the street, then glancing back at Ava.

"Yes," Ava said. "I got someone to cover my shift, but she hasn't shown up yet. We're not allowed to leave before our replacement shows up."

"So when's she coming?" I asked, turning around to face her.

"In half an hour. And that's not the only thing," Ava said,

scooting forward to be closer to us. "My mom called. She wants to visit me in Chicago. Can you believe it? She never goes anywhere, and all of a sudden she has to see Chicago? So what do I do?"

"What *can* you do?" I asked, thinking there weren't too many options here. Either her mom ended up in Chicago, completely mystified when she couldn't find Ava there, or else Ava told her where she really was.

"I could start driving to Chicago," Ava said. "Like, tonight."

"You could do that. Or you could just tell her that you gave up your internship and moved in with us," said Lucy.

"I don't think that would fly. I think if I tell her I've given up this really cool internship to work in a café, she's going to be livid." Ava sighed. "Come on, we could just go from here. All of us. Road trip. What do you say?" She pulled out a wad of dollar bills from her purse and waved it between us. "I've got gas and snacks money right here."

"Where did you get all that?" I asked. "Did you rob the place before you left? You're kind of acting a little wild."

"Mikayla, look at who you're talking about," Lucy said, with a small smile at me. The first one I'd seen in days. "Born to be wild?"

"I didn't rob anything!" Ava said. "I make this much

every day. Anyway, it's not that impressive. Mostly ones." She thumbed through the stack of bills. "Ooh! A ten! Score."

"Stop counting your money and just call your mom. She'll understand." Lucy pulled the car into a scenic overlook area. She parked the car and got out.

"Maybe. But I still don't want to tell her," Ava said as she climbed out of the backseat.

I followed her lead. "Just tell her. She'd want to know."

Lucy took a picnic basket out of the back of the small SUV. We followed her over to a rocky outcropping, overlooking the harbor below. The view of the islands, the harbor, and the sailboats below was amazing.

"This place is just gorgeous," I said, gazing down at a collection of lighthouses.

"I've probably never taken you guys here before, have I? This is one of my favorite spots in Bridgeport." Lucy set the basket on a flat rock and we all found seats around it, perching on boulders. "See, this is the problem. It's already July seventh. And *this* is the kind of stuff we should have been doing all summer. Instead, I got sucked into feeling bad about Jackson again, and then you started seeing him and I thought you'd done it on purpose, without thinking of me or my feelings, completely behind my back, which wasn't really true, and then you showed up—" She turned to Ava. "Well, you got here the day things turned weird."

"Hey. It wasn't my fault things got weird," Ava said, holding up her hands in self-defense. "There's no connection."

"I didn't mean that!" Lucy laughed. "I meant that we didn't have time to really get into the summer vibe before it all turned to high drama. And I hate high drama. That's my mom, not me. But I guess that old saying about the apple not falling far from the tree . . . I overreacted."

"Apple metaphors? Please," Ava said. "You've got to get out of that store now and then."

Lucy laughed. It was good to see her happy again—at least, I thought she was happy.

"I don't know if you did *over*react," I said. "What I did was a big deal. I just kind of froze. I felt like if I told you I'd met Jackson and thought he was, like, amazing, and we had this chemistry, you'd tell me not to go out with him. Because you still felt so weird around him. And why *would* I pick him, of all people? The answer is that I wouldn't. I didn't seek him out—I'd hung out with him a few times in groups before I even knew his name. I'd never felt like that about anyone before and I . . . I guess I made the wrong decisions. I tried to be up-front with you as soon as things really changed with Jackson, but I knew I should have talked to you before." I felt myself getting really emotional. I didn't want to cry, but I couldn't help myself.

"I see that now," Lucy said. "I just felt totally shocked and like you did the whole thing behind my back. I guess you were trying to be careful with my feelings, and I know you've been trying to apologize. I know it's taking me a long time to get used to the idea. But I think I'm there. Which is a good thing, because Jackson really likes you. He was telling me today how you broke up with him and now he's all mopey."

"Really?" That made me smile, despite my tears. Not that I wanted him to feel badly, but it was nice to know he missed me as much as I was missing him. I was a basket case. We'd only been broken up for a day.

Lucy reached over and brushed a few of my tears from my cheek. "Don't cry. I feel awful that this is my fault."

"It's not your fault," Ava said. "It's nobody's fault. It's just this freaky weird coincidence. But in a way, can't it be a happy coincidence?"

"Of course," Lucy agreed. "But the thing is, I need you guys to promise me something. From now on, let's always be really honest with one another about our feelings. I know— I'm the worst offender when it comes to this. I usually don't talk about my feelings. I usually try to hide them. But I've realized that doesn't work. For anyone, least of all me."

"If we're being honest here . . . then I should finally tell you about Chicago." She took a deep breath and stretched her arms above her head, leaning slightly from side to side, as if she was getting limbered up for ballet. "I guess I've been putting it off because it makes me seem like a complete idiot. I don't want you guys to look at me like that. I mean, other people can, and I really don't care. But you guys? No."

"We know you're not stupid," I said. "You get carried away sometimes, that's all."

"Yeah, well, this story will make you think differently," Ava said.

"We won't. I promise you." I smiled at her.

"What was so bad?" Lucy asked.

"Okay, so I show up to my internship. It's not much of an internship, it turns out. I have to get coffee for people, and lunch, and make a bunch of phone calls—"

"That's what internships are like, aren't they?" Lucy said.

"I guess. I didn't know that, though. So anyway, end of the week, turns out I didn't make a big important phone call and there was no reservation for this big lunch. My boss was furious with me. So to make it up to him, I booked the same party for that night—which was a major accomplishment. Yeah, and what does he do to thank me? He tries to hook up with me. Disgusting. So I quit. Problem was, I already spent all the money my mom gave me. I hadn't even paid my rent yet, so when I told my roommate about losing my job, she gave me, like, a day to come up with the money and then told me to move out. Which was okay, because she was really uptight."

"All this happened in one week?" Lucy asked. "Poor you—why didn't you let us know?"

"I was trying to figure it all out on my own. Turns out I pretty much suck at that," Ava said.

"That sounds like a horrible experience," I said. "I can't believe you didn't tell us before now. I mean, we could have come to your rescue or—or something."

"You guys have capes, right?" Ava joked. "You could fly in and do the whole superhero thing."

"But how did it all end up?" Lucy asked. "Are you really and truly okay? I kind of want to drive to Chicago tonight, just so we can tell that guy off."

"Oh, don't worry." Ava smiled ruefully. "I did that already."

We laughed. I'd seen Ava give people a piece of her mind. She could be pretty devastating when she wanted to be.

"Okay, now that we've got everything out in the open, let's toast." Lucy unscrewed the top of a tall glass bottle of sparkling lemonade and poured three cups full. "To friends. To summer. And to no more secrets." She handed me a cup and my gaze met hers. We both smiled.

"No more secrets." I tapped my cup against hers, and then against Ava's. "So spill where all this secret awesome food came from."

"Um, Gus," Lucy said.

Ava abruptly set down her cup. "Wait, didn't he give you food poisoning? Should we eat this stuff?"

"It's okay, he doesn't work for that caterer anymore. And he's really great." Lucy's face turned red and she laughed.

"He poisoned you, so you fell in love?" Ava said.

"Wait a second. How much have I missed in the last three days?" I'd never felt so out of the loop.

"It started before then . . . only I didn't realize it at the time. He kept coming by the store. I thought he was great, and I guess he liked me. We started hanging out, but I kept taking off when things got intense. For some reason he put up with me. Then we got stranded and we were super close, but then I took off again. . . . Anyway. I went by and fixed things. And he helped me make this picnic. So . . . I don't know if I'm in love, but I do like him. A lot."

"That's so great!" I said, squeezing her arm.

"That is, like, the vaguest story I have ever heard," Ava said. "I want details."

"Later," Lucy said. "But Mikayla, will you go ahead and tell Jackson it's okay and he doesn't need to mope around the store anymore, because I'm okay? Really."

"Are you sure?"

She nodded. "I told him I am, but it'll mean a lot more coming from you. He thinks you're perfect. You know, he might have acted like a rude dork back in eighth grade, but he's pretty nice now."

"He is," I agreed. I quickly grabbed my phone and sent a text to Jackson. *Hey. When can I see u?*

I don't know, Jackson wrote back.

Great. Now I had Jackson mad at me, just as Lucy had forgiven me.

Then my phone chimed with another message: *Later tonight when I get off work at WM?*

I smiled. I wanted nothing more than to see him that night. I couldn't wait to be in his arms again. But other things were more important right now, like friends, and reconnecting, and this wonderful-looking picnic, including the little crackers with strange cheese on them. But mostly friends.

I need to wait until tom'w, I wrote back. *But I promise I'll see you then.*

"Refill?" Lucy asked, holding the lemonade bottle over my cup.

"I'd love one," I told her, setting my phone aside.

"Okay, now that you guys are actually talking again

and might not kill each other, let's talk about this party we're having Saturday night," said Ava. "Who's in charge of entertainment?"

"*You*," Lucy and I said in unison.

CHAPTER 33

Lucy

You can do this.

I was heading up to the cabin after work, rehearsing my speech in the car.

Mom, this isn't going to work out. You can't pop in and out all summer planning your wedding and having me be your assistant. I have my life to live. This is going to be my amazing summer—who knows when I'll have one like this again, with my best friends? Not to mention Gus.

Just thinking that made me blush. *Focus, Lucy. Get through the speech and then you can think about Gus again.*

My mom had finally returned to Bridgeport, and she'd announced we were meeting with a couple of photographers after I got off work. Two at the most, she'd promised. They were Bridgeport's best and didn't I want to look at their work beforehand?

Never mind that I didn't have time to surf the Web and look at portfolios while I was at work. Gus had come by to meet me for lunch, bringing a strawberry smoothie for me, and we'd sat down by the water for fifteen minutes, talking and laughing, before I had to head back. So I guess you could say Mom's wedding was sliding even lower on my priority list.

Seeing Mom's white SUV in our driveway as I pulled up made me wonder if I really could do this. How could I say no to my mom? I'd been trying for years and it never stuck.

"Hey, Lucyloo," she greeted me when I walked into the house, which was empty save for her.

"Where are the photographers?" I asked.

"I canceled," she said. "I haven't seen you in days. The last thing we should do right away is look at photo albums." She gave me a hug. "So much has happened."

Tell me about it, I thought. "Let me guess. You sold another duplex?" I asked, eyebrow raised.

"Well, yes, how did you know?"

I shrugged. "I'm psychic? But—that's not the point." I set my bag on the kitchen counter and faced her. "Mom, I'm glad you're excited about your wedding. And I want it to be exactly what you want it to be. But this summer is a time for me, not a time for me to help you plan your second wedding, which if you think about it, probably shouldn't be as big of a deal as your first wedding—and I've spent so much time with you that I haven't—"

"Don't say another word," she said.

"Mom, just because you always want to talk about yourself and you won't let me talk—"

"I've decided to simplify," she said, interrupting me.

"Simplify," I repeated. Did Mom even know what that word meant?

"Gary and I have already decided on a different plan. He thought we were rushing too much, and actually, so did I. And then the food poisoning incident—I'm still sorry about that," she said. "Anyway, we'll get married at the orchard," she continued.

"Nana and Grandpa's apple orchard?" I asked, fairly stunned. "You will?"

"Not right now, of course. It'd be hot and buggy and nothing's in season," she continued. "No, we'll do it in the fall. Probably September, but maybe October. Have to get past bee season. I hate those bees. Always have. They just come around and look for fallen apples."

A bee in the tree is worth two in the hive, I thought, still not sure what that saying was supposed to mean. "Did you just say Oc-October?" I stammered. She was making this so easy. "Really?"

She nodded. "We want the trees to be full of fruit. We want the gorgeous fall weather. I'll have time to get the menu set, find a proper caterer, and all those good things."

Exactly what I'd been trying to tell her for the past month or more. Why rush something so important?

"And I know that I've been getting in the way around here," she said. "You have better things to do than hang out with me all the time."

"It's not—not that," I said. "It's just that you're rushing so much, and pulling me into all the decisions. I don't want to be the one who chooses stuff, Mom. I don't want that responsibility. It's up to you and Gary."

Mom nodded. "Very true."

"And there's so much else going on here. I mean, you have no idea . . ."

"I have some idea. For one thing, you and Mikayla are hardly talking—"

"Oh, no, we're past that," I assured her.

"For another, there's that boy from the caterer who really seems to like you and keeps showing up," she continued without acknowledging what I'd said.

"Gus," I said. "Yeah, he's—"

"And for a third thing, it seems like you and Jackson have kind of put things in the past. So if you just straighten out that situation with Mikayla, I'd say, all in all, not a bad summer so far. I feel completely fine leaving you here on your own."

"Mom. You're not listening to me! Mikayla and I are getting along fine," I said. "She and Jackson are a couple and things were weird for a while, but we got over it."

I was getting used to the fact that Jackson and Mikayla were together, and it wasn't because of Gus. It made sense for them to be together. Jackson had turned out to be a decent guy, and not the person I'd hated for the past few years because of a rumor I thought he'd helped get started. More importantly, he made my best friend really happy.

"Oh. Hm. Well, anyway, another reason I've got to take off is that the market's hot right now. I'm missing out. Kerri and Gary can't very well be the top team in our region if Kerri is two hundred miles away."

A few days ago, I probably would have muttered something like, "Right. The market. I should have known." But now, a part of me was kind of happy my mom hadn't totally changed. Plus, I realized I was getting exactly what I wanted. I should *thank* the real estate market in the Twin Cities. "So, Mom," I said instead. "That boy from Chef Michael's you just mentioned? Gus. We might be dating."

"Lucyloo!" Mom practically squealed with excitement. "Why didn't you say anything? Let's go out to dinner and you tell me all about it. Afterward I'll vanish, I promise."

"But . . . not totally, right?" I said. "You're still going to visit once or twice."

"If I can. And of course, I'll call now and then," she said.

Now and then? I nodded. "Of course." We headed out to her car, arm in arm. There was such a thing as speaking your mind—and things being better because of it.

That night, after dinner with Mom, I met Gus down at the beach. We went for a walk to check out the night sky, then spread a blanket on the sand and sat down next to each other, wrapping the blanket's edges around us.

He reached over for my hand as we both looked up at the sky. "That star right there?" he said, pointing with both our hands. "That one's called the Milky Way tart."

"Don't remind me of the samples disaster. Ever," I said, trying to pull my hand away. "Certain things should not be spoken of. Or sampled. In fact, when I get married—that is, *if* I get married—I'm having something simple, like Taco Bell, at the reception. In the parking lot. People get hot sauce packets for wedding favors."

"That's what your mom should have. Those Doritos Locos things!" Gus cried.

"What are you saying? My mom is crazy?" I asked. "I suppose she is obsessed with creating the perfect day. She should be on a reality show about weddings. It's going to be called *Say Yes to the Watercress.*"

"Watercress. I didn't even know what that was, until she insisted on it. I thought she was talking about having a reception on a sailboat," Gus said. "When the water *crested.*"

"You did not," I said.

"I did!" He held up his hands. "Scout's honor."

"Are you a scout?" I asked.

"No. Hey, I just thought of something. Since she's getting married at the orchard now, you'll have to have apples," he said. "Tons of apples. Bushels."

"Oh, definitely. I'll suggest Northern Spy apples. No, Haralson. Caramel-covered ones," I said. "Nobody will be able to eat them without ruining their clothes. It'll be *awesome.* Hey, speaking of parties, that reminds me. I was supposed to be hosting a bunch of epic parties this summer but I kind of got off to a slow start. So can you come to the first one, this Saturday night?"

"Wait a second. Isn't this epic enough?" Gus asked.

"It is for me." I looked at Gus and smiled. "Actually, this is pretty epic."

CHAPTER 34

Mikayla

Ava and I were chopping veggies in the kitchen about half an hour before the party was supposed to start on Saturday night. Lucy had taken off on a mission to get more ice; we'd already filled the fridge with cans and bottles of pop, juice, and Gatorade, but we realized we needed to fill some metal containers too. The only way Lucy's grandparents had approved the party was when we insisted that no one would drink—or do—anything illegal. They planned to enforce the rule by making an unannounced visit.

We had dip for the veggies, chips and salsa, mini cupcakes, and assorted other snacks on the kitchen counter and outside on the deck. The driveway had been cleared for a beanbag toss game, and we had a net up for badminton or volleyball games. There was croquet in the yard, but playing in the woods was going to be a challenge.

We'd invited about fifty people that we knew from our combined jobs, and encouraged Sarah, Henry, Gus, and Jackson to invite friends too. That might make this party too huge, but we'd lucked out and gotten a warm, gorgeous night.

Lucy walked in, carrying bags of ice. She dumped them on the counter. "I think I came up with the name for this place," she said.

Ava looked at me as she fanned out carrot sticks on a paper plate. "Uh-oh."

"No, it's good! I'm going to call it 'Cozy Charm,'" Lucy said.

I stared at her. "Seriously? No. You're not," I said.

"No, okay, you're right. Here, I already had a sign made. Hope you guys don't mind." She held up a giant paper plate, where she'd drawn a picture with a Sharpie pen and written *TIGER POD* in capital letters. "We just put this over the door as our crest."

Ava and I started laughing. "So we're finally in the Tiger Pod, huh? But we can't be tigers," I said. "We're turtles!"

"You know what? We're anything we decide to be this summer," Lucy said. "*That's* the whole point."

"Turtles don't scale! Turtles don't scale!" Ava cried,

lowering herself to the floor and looking pathetic.

We all started laughing hysterically.

"Plowed already?" Claire stood in the doorway, a set of small speakers in her hands.

"Hey, the DJ is here. Excellent!" Lucy said.

The two of them started setting up the music, and a few minutes later we were all dancing around the living room, jumping up and down. I hip-checked Lucy, danced a circle around Claire, followed Ava's moves. In a way, it didn't even matter if no one else showed up.

Then Henry, Sarah, and about twenty coworkers from the BBC walked through the open front door seemingly at the same time. Henry immediately jumped into the fray, dancing beside us. "Where've you been?" he yelled over the loud music.

"We brought your favorites!" Sarah announced, holding up boxes of the fancy chocolate-chip ice-cream sandwiches they served at the beach club.

"I love you guys," I said, hugging them both. "Thanks for coming!"

An hour later, Jackson and I were sitting on the deck together. We were smashed into a plastic Adirondack-style chair that wasn't technically wide enough for two. Other people were sitting on the deck, talking, laughing, and listening to music.

Off to the side, I could see and hear Gus and Lucy play-ing croquet in the woods. They were having so much fun together. Lucy was being bold and outgoing, challenging Gus and laughing with him at the same time, flirting and confident.

"It's absolutely true," I said. "I don't know why you don't believe me."

"No, it's not," Jackson said.

"Yes, it *is*," I insisted. "I could not talk to boys until I met you."

"No, I mean—you *still* can't talk to them. That's what I'm saying," Jackson teased as he squeezed me around the waist. "How about when I first met you and you said 'My fault it was. The stop sign I didn't see.'"

I narrowed my eyes at him. "Well, if you hadn't nearly run me over, maybe I would have been able to talk like a normal person," I said. "And don't forget what you said! 'Gosh, you really look terrible, can I take you to the hospital because you really look awful, and did I mention that you look horrible?'"

"I was trying to talk to you—" Jackson argued.

"Well, same here!" I cried.

"Wow. We were pretty hopeless. How did we ever end up together?"

"A series of unfortunate events," I said. "I mean, fortunate ones in the long run, but they involved multiple crashes and wounds, so . . . probably we should have stayed away from each other."

"Probably," Jackson agreed.

"That was a sign from the universe. Danger. Conflict approaching," I said.

"But what are we going to do?" Jackson asked. "It's too late now."

"Exactly," I said. "Way too late."

I turned to Jackson and hugged him closely to me. I didn't need to worry about meeting boys from now on. I'd already met the one I wanted to be with.

ACKNOWLEDGMENTS

How to Meet Boys came to light thanks to Farrin Jacobs, Jill Grinberg, and most of all Catherine Wallace, whose inspired thinking and editing made sure everything added up in a hundred different ways. Many thanks to all of you!

Also, my gratitude to the usual suspects: Sherren Clark, Erin Downing, Dawn Toboja, and Kristin Pederson. You knew I was terrible at meeting boys, but you never brought that up. Thanks.

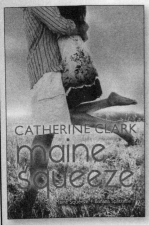
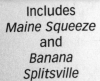

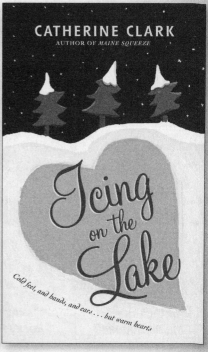

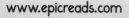